June Gloom

by Bronco Hammer

JUNE GLOOM
by

Bronco Hammer

First Edition
TITLE JUNE GLOOM
Print ISBN: 978-1-892798-38-1

Notice
The characters in this novel are fictitious. The characters, dialogue, products, places, and/or events in this book are creations of the imagination of the author or are used fictitiously. Any resemblance between the characters and events in this book and any person(s), living or dead, is purely coincidental. No product endorsements were given or provided in the development of this book.

Books by Bronco Hammer
Hollywood Scum Must Pay
Spank Me
JCPI
Pimps Must Die
Die You Commie Bastards
See You in Hell
Die You Filthy Animal
Man of Violence
I Stomp on your Throat
Dead Guy in the Alley, A Love Story
June Gloom

Friendship Foundation Books by Bronco Hammer
Die You Slimy Maggot
Deep State Deadly

Other books by Bronco Hammer
Assholes from Space
Narc in the Dark

Dedicated to Dave and Betsy
Thank you for your continuing defense of the thin blue line
Honest cops deserve a voice

Author's note:

This story is set in San Diego, California. I lived in downtown San Diego for several years at the City Front Terrace building in the Marina district and for a few years in the Gaslamp Quarter. For seven years, I had an office downtown. I know the neighborhood well, at least before the rapid decline. Several years ago, I moved to Coronado..

In Southern California, there is a seasonal coastal weather condition called '*May Gray*' and '*June Gloom.*' Our summer doesn't really start until the middle of July and runs to the end of October. During May and June, it is typically cool, foggy, and drizzly.

The protagonist in this story is former San Diego PD police officer June Glume. June is a ride-share driver. She takes notes on every ride. A portion of her journal appears at the beginning of most chapters. The journal entries have nothing to do with the story. They are simply color commentary depicting life on the streets of downtown San Diego.

Enjoy the story. Thank you for being a customer.

B.F. Hammer

Acknowledgements

John Coccillia — Ride-Share Advisor and Philosopher

Sami Jo Fife — Cover Model

Chris Jones — Men's Haberdashery Researcher and Police Consultant

Tim Fife — Truck Science and Manliness Technology Advisor

Jeff Trapp — Weapons Advisor and Violence Consultant

Kimberly Taylor — Road Manager Technology Advisor

Josh Williams — Choke Hold and Ass-kicking Consultant

Holli Lawton — Grammar and Words Advisor

Кимберли Кали — Canine Consultant and Leading Scientist

Scott Joseph — Chief Medical Officer and Cat Consultant

Mike Ratke — Hired Muscle

Randy Willard — Hired Muscle

Randy Lewis — Editorial Support

Justin Corvelo — Excavation Consultant (these bodies don't bury themselves)

Thank you for your help and input.

If I misrepresent something or make an error regarding the subject matter supported by my advisors, it is entirely my fault and should not reflect negatively on them. Following advice has never been my best thing.

(NOTE: No actual cats were harmed in the writing of this novel. A few goons didn't fare so well, but that's just business)

PREFACE

It was the closest shipping store.

The guy at the counter had to be a standard-issue failed ex-jock... I'm guessing the last notable achievement in his life was throwing a ball real hard in the 12th grade.

He eyeballed my body like a fat guy slobbering over a hot calzone.

Soft and flabby now, he no longer enjoyed being the school's hero, the coach's star, or the fantasy date of concupiscent cheerleaders. He sported a wristwatch with the logo of a professional football team, a belt with the logo of a professional basketball team, and contact lenses that caused him to involuntarily squint and crinkle his nose, as if he just detected a fart. My amateur diagnosis is that he probably had the lenses in the wrong eyes. His faded polyester polo shirt was stretched to the limits, accentuating his early middle-age, expanding midsection, which he was obviously trying to suck in as he spoke.

Who was this failed example of masculinity, you ask?

Just another random knob.

I've done business with these shipping joints before. I'd even been in this one before. The employees usually stand on the opposite side of the counter, maintaining a comfortable barrier of personal space between themselves and the customer. But this guy felt like he needed to come around the counter and stand beside me... a bit too close for any legitimate business purpose.

I didn't like it.

I'm not a prude, and I find no enjoyment or pleasure in discouraging men, even dorks. But all I wanted to do, all I could mentally *manage* to do after the week I just had, was mail some shit... just a damned box... I had to return an online order... Not that I'm *never* in the mood for a little give-and-take flirting, but right now I was definitely *not* in the mood for any bullshit from this fat mail-store Casanova.

I was wired up more than normal. I'd been up for four days straight doing my ride-share gig. The coffee, ephedrine, and two packets of stay-awake pills were still jacking up my perception of reality. I wasn't in any frame of mind to deal politely with for this turd's sexual innuendos. I was barely in control of my own bullshit. Oh yeah, I forgot the four cans of extreme alert drinks I slammed on my way here... no wonder I felt like ants were crawling up my legs.

"What's your first name, little lady?" Casanova mail guy said with an eyebrow wiggle.

I'm not little, I'm a lean and muscular five-foot-six. There are a lot of people in San Diego County who might say I'm not a lady either. I gazed at him through my pinpoint pupils... *shit*... *tunnel vision*... not that I couldn't focus, I was over-focused... I was looking at the world through an intensely bright microscope lens.

"June..." I mumbled, just wanting to get through this simple transaction and go home to crash.

"Last name..."

"Glume..."

Jock boy's face lit up. "Like June Gloom and May Gray? Like the months here in San Diego? That's funny," he snorted. The slob edged closer and touched my shoulder.

I took a deep breath.

He squeezed my shoulder, fingers pressing in like he was going to turn me towards him.

I chose not to jerk away. I turned into it and faced him head on.

"You know what else is funny?" I asked.

"No, sweet cheeks. What else is funny," he asked condescendingly as he slid his hand up and down the back of my arm as if it was a thing that was okay to do, an act that sealed his fate.

"This."

I shuffle-stepped back and snap-kicked him in the nuts.

It was funny.

Yes, I might be totally buzzed, but I haven't completely lost my sense of humor.

In fact, I'm hilarious.

Not so sure *he* liked my answer to his question, though. He puked on himself and lay twitching on the ground like a stuck pig.

When someone with a second dan in Shotokan karate snap kicks you in the gonads, you feel it. He knows that now. Good for him.

I decided to take my parcel to the shipping store across the street. My concern about any consequences from putting this wanker on the ground was low. He probably wouldn't press charges. Most likely, he sensed I would come back later and kill him if he did, and he would be correct in his thinking. Besides, a has-been jock will never admit a 'little lady' beat his ass.

So yeah, my name *is* June Glume. It's spelled G-L-U-M-E. I used to be a police department homicide detective here in sunny San Diego. Things didn't work out. Now I'm a ride-share driver.

I don't tolerate any shit.

Not from him.

Not from you.

Not from anybody.

You might want to take a step back.

Prologue

San Diego, California—Embarcadero

Stepping off the first commuter ferry from the Coronado Resort Hotel, the woman quickly made her way on foot to the meeting at the Emerald Tower. Her contact would do the hand-off to the courier. She realized she should have stayed downtown. But there were too many eyes downtown. No one would expect her to stay in Coronado. It was safer that way.

The woman glanced at her gold Cartier Santos watch. It was twenty before six in the morning. Frowning, she calculated she would be at the meeting on time only if she picked up the pace. Screw it, she'd call a ride-share. She tapped on her smart-phone and requested a pickup at the curve at Harbor Drive. The meeting with the courier was critical to getting the information back to Columbia. The nervous realtor hoped to buy his life with the information. He knew they went too far. But that wasn't her concern. The boss would deal with the messy stuff. Her job was to receive and verify the information.

She confirmed the ride-share and trekked forward.

This time of year, it was still pitch dark along the waterfront. The dense marine layer created a graveyard-cold mist, limiting one's vision to only a few feet at most. Stoically, she marched ahead, the staccato sound of clicking of her high heels imitating the deadened sound of a snare drum in a funeral march on the concrete. The beat of her walk was certainly brisker, but the dull soulless sound was unmistakably similar.

Obviously not a tourist, but perhaps a frequent visitor, she was well dressed, almost European. Sophisticated, but not overly so... her expensive, yet tasteful business attire was obviously designed to bond with the other wealthy citizens in the self-proclaimed America's finest city.

She sensed something. Business types, at least the good ones, are always a bit paranoid. It gives them an edge. She clutched her classic leather purse/valise combination tighter to her body, but not obviously so. Not tight enough to display fear, but tight enough to keep it secure in case of trouble.

The location, even though on a main drag, bore the distinctive aura of a threat. Nothing was there really, just dead space between points of interest... the type of pocket you find in a city where people feel okay about tossing litter, where no one is held responsible for anything... maybe fifty yards... like every city has sprinkled across the downtown areas. Not bad enough for cops to be there, but not safe enough to loiter for long. Fast walk... get through... ignore.

Near the old aircraft carrier museum and her hotel destination, she found herself in this no-man's-land. Maybe a sleeping bum was nearby on one of the park benches... it was too foggy to see. She walked faster.

She might have been late thirties or early forties. Most men would consider her quite attractive. The light blue leather jacket, the short black skirt, the tall heels, not stripper heels but absolutely not matronly by a long shot... with her lean figure, custom rack, and the very pricey highlights in her brownish-blonde hair, she stood out. Her look was noticeably different from the typical downtown San Diego cubicle chick whose focus is on comfort and ease of morning commutes rather than their appearance as they plod along the sidewalk to their downtown office job. Clearly, this woman was a C-level player in the business world.

Her movements were graceful yet with purpose, as she marched briskly towards the resort hotel that was hosting her potential clients, ignoring her sense of discomfort about walking alone.

She was startled by a voice that was unexpectedly close...

Uncomfortably close.

"Hey lady!"

She slowly turned, smiling a patently fake and condescending smile as she faced him. She knew how to handle aggressive panhandlers. Be assertive... put them in their place.

Instead of a street beggar, she saw someone local to San Diego, dressed like a bum. Someone she did business with.

The shooter smiled back and pressed the trigger. His sawed-off shotgun's muzzle erupted into an orange flame.

The woman flew backwards, collapsing on the concrete in an

awkward sprawl. No longer beautiful. No longer sophisticated. Just a slab of well-dressed bloody meat on concrete.

Assessing the kill, the shooter concluded that the home-made sound suppressor worked well enough. The report from the weapon was loud, but not the thundering blast one would expect when firing a twelve-gauge by the water near the Embarcadero. A shotgun is good for point-blank work, or for leaving a message. Here, the shooter had both on the agenda.

Bending over the dying woman, the murderer callously retrieved a document from the dead woman's expensive leather valise, then casually walked away... taking just a few steps before pausing and catching a quick glimpse back at the scene. The woman's body was still twitching... but she was done. The weapon accomplished its intended job.

Another one dead... others to follow...

The shooter continued walking east at a controlled pace, brisk but not fast enough to attract attention. Crossing Harbor Drive, the killer broke the weapon down while on the move and stuffed it in a carry-on bag.

A two-block walk... Call for a ride-share. Cabs and cars hovering around the train station... the Amtrak just arrived, its passengers flooding out onto the street.

This one was easier than I thought it would be... Lost in the crowd. Clear the area... Freedom.

CHAPTER 1

Ride share journal entry—June Glume

I hit a drive through for coffee before getting my second early morning ride-share passengers, a nice middle-aged couple just getting off the plane from some town in North Dakota... or one of the Dakotas... Are there two Dakotas? Who would possibly care? No one goes there on purpose. Wasn't one of them known as the Cheese State? Or was that someplace else? Cheese is good.

The lady passenger is a heavy-set woman... She looks like she ate her fair share of cheese. But what's the proper term now? Full figured... that's it. She is generously full-figured... and so is her husband. The wife is wearing a flowered muumuu, and he is sporting an Aloha shirt, cargo shorts, white sox, and a pair of brown men's leather oxfords. They will definitely blend in nicely with the local SoCal scene.

But I'm not judging. How can I? I've been wearing the same outfit for three days. I have no room to criticize anyone else, but at least I don't stink yet... that much.

I casually raised my hand to conceal my face and took a whiff.

Hell, I *do* stink.

Self-consciously, I subtly opened the glove box and retrieved my spare air freshener. I subtly ripped it open... much better.

The happy pair rambled on, chattering about how warm it was... dipshits. Do they have any idea how annoying that can be? I've been freezing my ass off. It's still below sixty degrees this morning and I've been cold all night, driving drunks around until about four, then getting breakfast. After that, I started picking off some tourist trips at the airport. It got close to the low fifties last night.... Where's the National Guard when you need them? Typical bullshit winter weather. Warm? No, it's shitty with an increasing chance for more cold-assed shittiness throughout this seemingly never-ending Southern California winter. That old Sinatra song about the tramp lady was right. California is definitely too cold and too damp. I hate it here too right now. Damned chilly-assed weather.

But the chill doesn't seem to bother my passengers. They were *Dakota tough.* Is that a thing? It makes sense. The weak couldn't survive in a place like that. The chubby couple sit happily chatting away with each other, each pointing out the sites along Harbor Drive as they spot them... Coast Guard office, Harbor Island Marina yachts, Star of India.... Thankfully, they just talk to each other. I'm not in the mood for talking. I've had enough talking. My job is simply to drive them from the airport to the interestingly named Ocean Breeze Inn, an aging sixty or seventy-year-old relic in need of a good wrecking ball. It was situated between high-rises, with Little Italy on one side and the County complex on the other.

I guess being close to the bay was like being close to the ocean, and there was a slight breeze as the prevailing coastal wind funneled and built itself up into bruising gusts as it squeezed through the streets and alleys of the city. But the whole concept of ocean breezes and beaches is probably not in the cards for these two lovebirds. I always thought of the beach and the city as two completely different things, and downtown isn't a vacation at the beach. Downtown is a rookery of filth and crime.

Arriving at their destination and I pull into the handicap spot to let them out. The old hotel wouldn't be there forever. A three-story motor inn from the fifties just couldn't bleed the full value out of the ground it stood on for the owners. Eventually, it will get bulldozed and replaced with another high-rise that will charge rates far beyond the means of these people... but that's life in the city. At least it's better than Hotel Circle… maybe.

I got out and helped them with the bags. Their little vacation getaway spot was not exactly a jewel. The Ocean Breeze Inn amenities included most rooms adjacent to the railroad tracks, never-ending street level noise from drunk and stoned partiers in Little Italy, and zero natural California sunlight. The surrounding high-rise towers blocked out the sun, creating a gray shadow world on the street below... and leaving the little three-story motor inn nestled in eternal darkness.

For visitors with a discerning olfactory sense, the neighborhood provides the unique ambiance of unconscious bum stank effervescing throughout a block swathed in a haze of urine smell and vomit... every few feet another cardboard sign marked another pathetic street dreg's personal territory, every doorway was a hobo bathroom, and every alley provided sufficient privacy for ten-or-twenty-dollar sex acts by the prostitutes of every persuasion and perversion who populate the downtown area.

This couple doesn't seem to care, though. I guess next to Bismarck, North Dakota in January, downtown San Diego is just a slice of heaven.

Enough is enough... The pair of gawking tourists will be the last downtown passengers for this work binge. I am coming off the buzz of my drugs. I'm starting to feel depressed. Downtown will do that to you.

I headed towards home to try my luck on Coronado... I could probably take a few sailors to and from the Irish Pub before calling it a day. Then finally, I could get some sleep. Perhaps it would require codeine to counteract the uppers, but I need rest. Three days straight behind the wheel is enough... or has it been four? ... more later...

- End journal entry

Coronado Island

I parked my car in the designated parking spot behind the apartment building adjacent to the alley. It was over. Another power-shift of ride-share driving completed.

Some of my neighbors might describe me as an athletically built woman in tight black jeans, a black t-shirt, and a black leather blazer. Others might describe me as a burn-out lunatic recluse creeping around the area. Either one might be correct. I trudged up the stairs to my F Avenue apartment, pausing to take in a deep breath of clean salt air as I reached the small deck at the top... I leaned over the railing and gazed across the bay. The view down the alley was magnificent, as usual, the downtown San Diego skyline, the big bay... I paused for one more calming breath, breathing in through the nose and out through the mouth like the shrink showed me, and I enjoyed a brief moment of *not* gazing into hectic city traffic in front, behind, and beside me. It had been three solid days of driving. Now I needed to take a few days off. Thank goodness for coffee and ephedrine, the secret formula I developed while working the night shift as a San Diego PD detective... at least before I got fired. Maybe I should have stayed in the Army. Maybe I should have… to hell with it… *should-a-could-a-would-a*… that's a dangerous game I don't want to get in the habit of playing. I'm doing fine.

I'm living on Coronado Island.

Suck it, world.

Living above somebody's garage might seem like a half of a step above skid row to most posh sophisticates, but not here on our little resorts and Navy dominated island. A little apartment home above a garage in Coronado, if you can find one, it is more pleasant than most of the ocean front beach houses you find up and down the coast. At least in my opinion.

Most of those beach houses, no matter how elegant, usually have a short-term rental place, or worse yet, one of the notorious online home-hotel services, operating on either side of them. We can thank the trust fund babies for that. The endless stream of nouveaux-transient neighbors meant that on most nights, your ten-to-thirty-million-dollar dream beach mansion would probably be surrounded by noisy drunk partiers from Phoenix and Tucson. Or if things were *really* dismal, you are blessed with a rotating horde of obnoxious east-coast dickheads to deal with all summer. I hate those guys. The wealthy east coast tourists seemed oblivious to the fact that nobody else in the country gives a shit about New York, or Philadelphia, or worse yet, that pathetic shithole Baltimore… smug pricks. So tired of hearing that you can't get a pizza here at three AM… seriously?

So, the proud owners of the expensive ocean-front estates on the sand get to experience an ever-evolving daily or weekly chain of new neighbors who sit outside their weekly/monthly rental house smoking pot, getting puke-level drunk, and blasting Springsteen on boom-box sub-woofer stereos at six in the morning, all while ruining the beach ambiance for the locals. I hate Springsteen. He is such a pussy.

The online renters are often total assholes, which is the most despicable of the variety… or at least they are total assholes during their vacation. They might be nice otherwise… but I couldn't find it in my heart to blame them very much. If I could swing a week of getting drunk and stoned on the beach, I might go for it too. Especially if I could bring along a decent guy, one who knew what to do to please me and knew to leave when I was finished with him... and to never call back.

I pushed the pointless real-estate drama out of my head and retrieved the keys from my pocket with my right hand. With the precision of a surgeon, I inserted the heavy gold colored Schlage key in the lock, slowly and silently twisting the key. Out of habit, I drew my weapon with my left hand. I held it close to my body, ready to smoke anyone who tried to grab it. You never know, even on a low crime island like Coronado. Anybody inside who wasn't supposed to be there was going to get shot in the face. There wasn't supposed to be anyone there. I live alone and do not care for guests.

Instinctively, I reacted to the potential threat. I felt my eyes focus and my hands steady… the cop instinct kicked in. My stretch in the military trained my body and mind to flash into a hyper-vigilante state of readiness. I was in my happy place. I almost hoped there was some rat bastard in there with nefarious intent. The drugs were still jacking me up. I wanted to kill someone. Or get killed. Either way was good.

Opening the door, I looked around, eyeballing the room for any telltale signs of intruders, and quickly determined nothing seemed disturbed. Even after being out of the cop business for all this time, I retained enough tactical experience to know that nothing is certain, and things aren't always as they appear. I took my time, carefully clearing the entire apartment... twice... checking every closet and hiding place. There was no choice... something told me, insisted; I had to check everything... all the time...

This isn't a compulsion, I told myself.

This is normal.

Check everything.

Someone could be there.

Only a fool wouldn't check.

Nothing… Satisfied my home was clear, and that I was at long last alone, I hung the Glock 26 on the nail above the door, keeping it easy to grab should an asshole try to force entry. Not that there were many assholes pulling that shit on Coronado. That was more of a downtown San Diego or Oceanside thing, places where assholes free range with the blessing of the commie loving city hall shit fucks... politicians... scumbags. Just the thought of those lying pricks compelled me to fast walk to the bathroom and spit in the toilet...

I went to the bedroom. Sitting down on the bed, I yanked my Rocky 911 boots off my feet, jerked the thick smelly black socks off, and slid out of my jeans. I carefully hung my leather jacket on a hook behind the bedroom door, then tugged my shirt over my head and undid my bra. Gathering my soiled work clothes, I placed the smelly bastards in the hamper for laundry day... or maybe I should just burn them like a biohazard. That might be better.

I wish I had a flamethrower...

That's a thing I wish sometimes.

I think they're illegal here in California.

Flamethrowers and wishes.

One illegal and the other pointless and unattainable.

Sad.

I went in the bathroom and flicked the faucet in the tub to boil-level heat. I stepped into the old eagle claw tub, lifting the lever and blasted skin-reddening hot water on my head, spraying down from above. The quick hot shower washed the visible city stink off of me. I drenched myself in liquid soap and rinsed. I repeated that process four times.

Wrapping a microfiber bath towel around me, I wandered back to the bedroom. I tugged on some denim shorts, tube top, pulled on a local brewery tank top, and scooted my feet into some leather flip-flops... A quick work-to-beach-life conversion. I almost felt human, at least sort of like the rest of the humans... as human as possible for me.

A short walk over to the Central Liquor Store for a resupply of rum and a couple of deli sandwiches came next. Then on the walk home, I checked my street side mailbox. All done. My morning tasks now complete.

I envisioned mixing up a big batch of rum and orange juice, disguising the concoction in a fake plastic iced-coffee cup, and then heading for the sand. Afterwards, with the help of two or three off-the-shelf pain relievers and a handful of sleeping pills, maybe I'd get a couple of days of sleep. Life is good.

I prepped my beach booze and headed for the door when I felt the vibration of an incoming call from the cell phone in my pocket. I looked at the caller ID... Rose, my former colleague from the San

Diego Police Department homicide unit.

We worked patrol together.

That used to mean something.

I don't think it does anymore.

"Yeah?" I grunted.

"June... it's Rose... Bad news..." It was the lugubrious voice of my ex-partner in homicide.

"Now what?" My attitude quickly jammed gears from the chill zone to the pissed-off zone. What had it been... two years? No, it had been a couple of months since Rose texted. I had ignored it like always. Even so, it seemed like the only time anyone initiated any kind of human interaction with me was to announce that the world was about to take a giant shit on good old June Glume. Or did Rose seem exceptionally irritating because of the abrupt end of my amphetamine/caffeine binge and the uncomfortable delay in launching my alcohol binge? It was probably both. I did a quick self-assessment... my hands were shaking, and my neck and jaws ached... still fucked up.

There was a red plastic disposable cup on the counter. It looked clean enough. I poured a half glass of rum in it and quickly slugged it down.

Rose was the closest thing I still had to a friend in the police department, but I would be happy to never hear from her again for the rest of my life. Friendship is an overrated institution, I thought. *Where were these so-called friends when I needed help? Where were these pricks when I got thrown under the bus like a piece of shit maggot by my fellow brothers and sisters in blue?*

I pushed aside my inner dialogue and succumbed to my curiosity, asking, "Now what?"

"Another dead woman... a homicide on the Embarcadero... in that tiny no-man's-land between the old Seaport Village and the Broadway Pier... just beyond the new bum park. Some classy looking rich bitch downtown on business... Messy." Rose spoke in her typical staccato sound bites.

I felt my irritation festering. "So why are you telling me this shit?" I knew there was a point coming and it would probably be a pointed stick in the eye.

Rose continued, "Her cell phone indicated she just called for a ride-share. Her driver found the body."

I frowned. Another ride-share related murder... that made it five this year. Not that I followed this shit anymore. "So... who did it?"

"Unknown perp... no description, no evidence at the scene worth anything, no worthwhile ballistics, nothing."

Man, I wished she'd get to the point. "... And you think I give a shit *because*?" I was growing very weary of this conversation. I needed a drink.

"The woman was in your car two weeks ago, June. You gave the victim a ride. You met her. Hot, blonde, a very well-maintained forty, foreign national. Columbian."

I consider myself a measured woman, careful not to betray fear or panic, but that detail made me involuntarily suck in a breath. Somehow, I instantly recalled the woman and the ride.

Hell... I *did* know her.

Psychic flash?

No, that paranormal stuff is bullshit.

Still, I knew the victim. I couldn't explain how, but with only hearing those words, I remembered in stark detail the woman that just a few seconds ago I had completely forgotten. Cop instinct? Do people who are about to be murdered have an aura about them that only an old street cop can see? Is it some unknown mental force that files them away inside a subconscious vault of crime data living inside your head?

No... I knew that if not for substance abuse, I would have near photographic recollection of everything I ever saw or heard. It was an affliction, not a blessing, but it was an affliction that made me a near mythical detective on SDPD before my shooting a few years ago. Now my uncanny ability to recall even the slightest details from the past was simply another physically painful annoyance, like tinnitus or gout. The only effective treatment was drugs and booze.

Slowly, I walked to the kitchen as I listened to Rose whine about the evidence-free crime scene. I snatched a pain pill out of one of my pill bowls in the cabinet. I broke it in half and popped it in my mouth before tossing the other half back into the bowl. Regular pill bottles disgust me. I don't know why. So I use bowls.

As Rose blathered, I remembered something else. The ride-share pickup was at a coffee shop in the Marina District near the trolley station, that old brick place. The woman appeared well-dressed. Maybe a lawyer, or at least the lawyer type. Interesting but subtle accent. She had a bit of *'queen bitch of the universe'* attitude about her. Her face was in decent shape for a forty-something and her hair had to cost her at least three hundred bucks to be that perfectly blonde and highlighted. She was hot for a middle-aged broad. I'm not gay, but I had a feeling that *this* woman could possibly turn me that way. She had that intense prurient vibe about her...

Steamy?

Yeah... she was steamy... but ice cold at the same time.

I recalled her big leather briefcase/ purse combination. It seemed heavy... and she spoke with that accent... At the time, I thought she might be from Mexico City, but now that I think about it, because I didn't give a shit at the time, it was South American. Mostly I remembered the three-star rating I got from that cheap-assed old bag. It pissed me off. Not that it mattered. But… pride.

I began losing my train of thought as the meds kicked in. I tried to recall more detail about the woman, the scene, any conversations, but I could only focus on the cheap rating... was that another obsession? Is obsession what the shrink would call it? Fuck the shrink. The shrink is an asshole. This is business. I tried to remember... focus, June… remember.

The drive was textbook... I recollected the details as I reconstructed the experience in my mind as if I was dictating a report... I was polite, fairly sober, and got her to her destination expeditiously. The passenger said little. I recall her focusing on a document. Reading a piece of paper in the back of a ride share was odd in a digital world... a digital world in which this asshole rich bitch gave me a fucking three. A mediocre rating was undeserved and was bullshit... assholes! Everyone is an asshole! The victim was an asshole.

Shit. I was off the track again... probably the meds and rum.

I tried harder to focus. Where did I take this woman? Oh yeah, she asked to be dropped near a dive bar in Little Italy, so when we got there, I pulled over and let her out in front of the bar. The woman looked out of place. Something was wrong. I remembered. The lady went through the usual motions of someone who doesn't want to be seen. She walked away with her head down, quick peeking out of the corners of her eyes as she moved, hiding behind oversize sunglasses, and nervous... exceptionally nervous. I remembered wondering at the time what was in that big bag.

I remembered she asked me something. She asked me about alternatives to staying downtown. I told her about the Marriott across the bay, the water taxi, and the commuter ferry. I also mentioned Harbor Island. But I didn't think she listened to me.

Rose finished talking about the same time I finished tuning her out.

"Can you help me out with this?" Rose asked as she braced herself to get blasted again by her volatile ex-partner.

I was curious, but I never forget how I was backstabbed by the city. I spat venom. "Fuck you. I'm glad she's dead. I wish you were dead too."

I abruptly disconnected... *fuck Rose... fuck the police department... fuck the Chief... the treacherous, disloyal prick cowards. I'm going to the beach.*

CHAPTER 2

Ride share journal entry—June Glume

"Welcome to San Diego."

I said it, but I didn't mean it. I hate hipsters. For some reason, they believe they are so particularly good at being alive. I hold them accountable for the stupid IPA scourge that is destroying the country's pubs and breweries. They are responsible for neck beards and skinny jeans. They are also guilty of impersonating lumberjacks... most of their women look like lumberjacks too, or else failed Stevie Nicks clones. I'm not sure which is worse.

This pair I have in the back of my car just disembarked off an inbound flight from Nashville, Tennessee.

They are insisting on making clear to me that are professionals. The dude even told me when I opened the trunk for his suitcase... "I'm a professional." He mentioned it again when he climbed into the back seat, acting under the assumption that I give a shit.

I guess professionals are now skinny fuckers who do business in starched flannel shirts, wide suspenders under their sport coat, skinny jeans, and mountain climbing boots. I noticed that the woman with him didn't shave her armpits. She is wearing some sort of frumpy cotton dress, carrying a jean jacket with a Lana Marks Cleopatra Clutch, and sporting a pair of Miu Miu Crystal Embellished Patent Leather Pumps. She reminded me of a turd with glitter sprinkled on it, not that I have ever seen a turd with glitter sprinkled on it, but if I ever do, I will probably think of her.

The woman sat quietly as her lumberjack dude does all the talking. He pulled a tablet computer thingy out from his blue canvas briefcase before we left the curb, making bold little finger swipes on it like he's a virtuoso of... screen swiping... Is that a thing? I don't know, he just looks like a pretentious ass who is finger painting on a plastic toy.

As we roll out of the airport, I attempt again to confirm with him that we are going to the Hyatt on Harbor, but he is determined to ignore me. They both had their expensive little wireless earpieces in and were intently focused on watching something on the tablet computer.

Then I realized he wasn't ignoring me; he simply couldn't hear me. I reached back and waved my hand in the general area of his face.

"What?" he asks sharply as he yanks out an earpiece, clearly pissed off that I disturbed their shared enjoyment of some stupid video as we cruised along the scenic San Diego Bay. He put the tablet flat on his lap. I glanced back and noticed the video was a clip from one of those punk-assed commie late-night talk show hosts chattering on about some commie bullshit. I hate commies. But at least I had his undivided attention now.

"Just confirming the Hyatt as our destination," I said it as calmly as I could. I felt my hands doing the tremor thing. I was either more buzzed than I thought, or ɨ my central nervous system was amping up and sensing that an ass beating would soon be on the agenda. Either one was fine with me.

"It's the address I put in the app. Just drive the car. Try doing your job, okay? I don't have time for this. I'm a professional."

What an asshole. Stupid hipster... Tremors increasing. Blood pressure cranking... Calm, calm, calm.... ohhmmmm... Namaste... We are all one with the universe...

Fuck yoga crap. I want to beat this prick's ass.

I took them to the Hyatt on Harbor. We got to the front door, and they bailed before I could get out of the car to open the door for them. There was a momentary delay as they wandered off without their bags. I flashed a raised eyebrow, sharing a *'what ya gonna do'* look at the valet, who acknowledged my gesture with a surreptitious shrug and an eye roll.

Suddenly, hipster and hipsterette came bouncing out of the lobby, appearing outraged and put upon.

"You took us to the wrong Hyatt!" the woman spat out accusingly, clearly fuming at my incompetence.

It was kind of funny, actually; she started vaping the second she stepped out of the car, and it looked like she was literally fuming, with vape steam or whatever that shit is coming out of her nose. I almost laughed.

Mister hipster tagged in next. He was obviously the negotiator of the two. He wasn't angry at me, but he addressed me as if he was patiently correcting an errant child. "We need to stay here... but apparently, we were somehow incorrectly booked at the Mission Beach Hyatt, and now this one is booked up." He said it like it was my fault.

I was loving it. "Oh no, I'm so sorry," I lied... and attempted to smile... I'm not good at smiling. I don't think they bought it.

The female yanked her vape thingy out of her mouth like a soldier pulling the pin of a grenade with his teeth in an old war movie and then proceeded to go off on me. "I don't care for your deportment," the woman said, shaking with anger, disgust, and a bunch more *'how dare you'* style dramatic facial expressions.

Personally, I don't care for having my deportment slandered, but I played it cool and laid some verbal judo on them, the negotiating tactic I learned in my cop days. "So, I hear you telling me you were booked into the wrong hotel? Who booked the reservation?" I asked, already knowing the answer.

This was fun.

It was his turn to stick his mug in my face. "That doesn't matter," he barked, attempting to take his own error off the table as a debating point.

Clearly, they had a future in the democrat party.

"Actually, it does matter, paper towel lumberjack dude. Sounds like you fucked up."

I got back in my car, put it in gear, and split... sticking my hand out the window and giving them the finger as I drove back onto Harbor Drive. In retrospect, I don't think the lumberjack paper towel reference registered in his little internet addled professional brain.

I glanced back in the mirror. No doubt he was in the process of giving me a one rating on his phone. Jerks. I quickly gave them the worst possible passenger rating as I steered with my knees. *Pricks... Assholes... Jerk hipster asshole pricks.*

- End journal entry

San Diego PD Homicide - Downtown San Diego

"What did she say?" Sergeant Daryl Bridges was curious. He wasn't crazy about even *knowing* Glume, or as the other detectives of her era called her, June Gloom… like the dense foggy marine layer that hangs over the city in May and June that perfectly reflected the ex-cop's personality. Bridges saw Glume to be a high-risk informant, not a cop, not even an ex-cop, just another dirtbag snitch.

Bridges eyeballed the weary detective in front of him.

Reliable Rose, as their division commander called her, looked like she had been on the job for forty years instead of fourteen. She was still mildly attractive when she wanted to be but her usual attire, a cheap and ill-fitting mannish brown suit over a bargain-basement beige blouse with scuffed-up manly looking tie shoes made her look like a woman who didn't care about herself anymore. Still, Rose was one of the more responsible detectives in homicide. Most of the cops there didn't give a shit any longer since the commie brigade took over the political scene. Between the whole anti-cop movement spreading over Southern California and the crooked state and local politicians and the police chiefs who dreamed of a future career in politics, what little motivation that was left to do a good job had been totally destroyed.

But old Rose thought little about morality, just her case load. She was… reliable.

Rose Lopez frowned and made a funny wrinkling movement with the skin above her nose like a squint but meant to show frustration, or perhaps a deep thought, as she answered her boss's question. "She told me to go fuck myself."

"Shit," Bridges muttered and twitched in an overly dramatic display of disgust. "I got bodies stacking up downtown. I need results, Rose, not obstruction of justice from an asshole ex-cop."

The side of Rose's mouth turned down in a determined expression and shook her head, "No, boss… you don't get her… that means she is *thinking* about it. She would have just hung up immediately if she wasn't interested. Juney is a little rough around the edges. You just got to get to know her. You never worked with her on the job."

"Bullshit Rose. I know all I need to know. Your pal '*Juney*' is a drug addict, alcoholic, deranged loner, violent psycho, and a scumbag."

"Just because of the shooting?" Rose spoke in a combination statement, question, observation, so she retained some deniability about defending June.

"The shooting… and she got that dirtbag Raven dude off the murder charge. I know she torpedoed that case intentionally."

"Raven? The Delta Force guy? He didn't do it."

"And you still don't know who did… But I do. I *know* it was him. He's an asshole. We had a scalp for that murder and she let him go."

Rose was smart enough to restrict her loyalty to her friend but not extend any support to her friend's friends. She paused for a moment like she was considering the wisdom of her supervisor before jump-starting her defense of Glume.

"Well… maybe, but she has some redeeming traits too," Rose responded, her words sounding a smidgen more defensive than she meant them sound. Rose always considered June her closest friend in the department, at least before Glume managed to get herself fired over that shooting. Not that she shouldn't have been fired. Someone had to be fired. City hall wanted a scalp, and they couldn't find a white heterosexual male to blame… so the next best thing was a white heterosexual female… especially one who told the mayor to go suck her dick when the finger-pointing started, which was coolest burn ever, but definitely career ending. It wasn't like she didn't have a history of conflict with elected officials. There was the time she booked a county commissioner for contempt of cop. And that nutty councilman still is out to get her. Rose frowned… Glume has a lot of enemies and few friends.

Bridges wasn't buying Rose's concerns. "Name one thing, Rose… Really, tell me *one* good thing about June Fucking Gloom," Bridges challenged.

"She is always on time… she never dawdles… She can remember everything she sees and hears, it's almost creepy… and she is *very* organized." Rose's face revealed she knew she didn't have much. That brief list of positive attributes was about it. Sure, there *were* other things, but those qualities were difficult to articulate, and the boss, a likely candidate for a 'Toxic Male Magazine' cover shoot, wouldn't understand.

My shit is weak here, Rose realized.

Bridges ramped up his anger. "And that makes up for the rest of her shit?" Bridges' skepticism was in high gear. He enjoyed proving points. It was like a competitive game to him, and he might be on the verge of a crushing victory.

Rose tried again. "Maybe there is more good stuff, but I just can't think of it right now... she's good people, boss. Why do you have to be so judgmental?" Rose spewed counteraccusations and vague bullshit; both were considered top defensive moves in modern police agencies whenever the boss was pissed off.

Bridges frowned. Or maybe it was a sneer. "I'm a cop... I'm paid to be judgmental so normal society can enjoy giving everyone else the benefit of the doubt and feel all warm and fuzzy about themselves... Glume is a dirtbag... if she calls back treat her like any other snitch. Keep a tight leash on her. I don't trust her."

"You don't trust anybody," Rose spewed one more lame accusation, knowing it was a loser before she said it. Hell, Bridges took pride in not trusting anyone. She was starting to get pissed off... she tried to restrain the urge to tell her boss to go blow it out his self-righteous ass.

He took a deep breath and gave her his highly developed *'you're a dumbass'* look. "Did you miss the part where I mentioned that I'm a cop?"

Rose knew that little slap of sarcasm was meant to demean her being a *real* detective. She was as bad-ass as any other cop, she just wasn't a pretentious dickhead about it, like her cranky-assed sergeant. Rose really wanted to call him a woman-hater, but she couldn't do that and be fair. He hated all the men too... so that little chunk of outrage quickly fizzled. He was just being Bridges, and he was a really outstanding detective sergeant, just a shitty human being. She took a deep breath and tried to start over, this time pulling a sincerity arrow out of her quiver of debate tactics.

"We're *all* cops here, boss... June just got lost after the shooting... she isn't the same person anymore."

Bridges considered her words. He responded with the fact... a cold and brutal fact. "She got a hostage shot."

Back on defense, she responded calmly, "She killed the perp... and a bagman, too. And nobody was mad at her when she took out that escaped rapist six years ago."

"The rapist? She beat that bastard to death with her bare hands."

"It was a fight... Sometimes these things happen. The hostage thing just happened too. June is a good person at heart."

Bridges didn't want to continue with this pointless debate. He decided that he already won and didn't want to talk about it anymore, but Rose looked like she had more to say.

Bridges cut her off and re-engaged with a fury before she could speak. "So what?" He began dramatically counting off on his fingers as he ticked off the June Glume hit parade of fuck-ups. "That dead hostage doesn't give a shit if she's a good person. The dead hostage's family doesn't give a rat's ass if June Glume is a good person. Our mayor hates her insubordinate guts. The department forked out nine million to settle the suit. That payout was our raise for the next ten years, Lopez. She's an asshole!" His face turned red, and his voice hit the threshold volume allowable before HR would step in and spank him with another excessive rudeness charge, or whatever the hell it was called when you yelled at your subordinates.

Knowing when to shut the fuck up and walk away wasn't Rose's best thing. "That's not on her..." she elaborated. "Insurance kicked in after a million. The city had to pay a one million, not nine million."

"So?"

Rose suddenly realized the discussion was way off the rails again, and she was about to step into a world of hurt. She tried to hit the brakes with another vague response, intended to de-escalate her boss's pending rage induced stroke. "So... I'm just saying," she bleated out in a half-hearted whine.

They stared at each other for a full thirty seconds. The veins in Bridge's neck were slowly receding back into his flesh. His face was resuming his normal skin tone. She thought it was over. Rose hoped it was over. She hoped he would walk away.

He started to turn away... maybe he's finished, she hoped. She might even be able to call this discussion a draw later when she told her husband about it.

Then the Sergeant spun back around and lost his cool again, shouting in her face, "Dead fucking citizen, Rose... A dead as fuck citizen!"

She stepped back, realizing she should have just shut up in the first place. Why did she press this guy? Dammit... It's so hard not to talk. But... shit. She felt her chin tremble... oh no, she wouldn't let this jerk make her cry... she'd never outlive that shit. She went back on active defense, "Quit shouting. I get it. Gawd... you know, you can be a real... never mind." Time for a tactical retreat. Why was she even defending June? She didn't really know. June wouldn't defend her. June didn't care about anybody.

"Say it." Bridges demanded.

He was still hot under the collar. Rose saw he had that jaw thing going that looked as if he was preparing to rip a bite out of a big hunk of meat like a cave dweller eating a raw dinosaur leg. Rose surrendered, lowering her head and turning away. "I'll update her snitch jacket. She'll call back." She obediently turned away from him this time and slinked back to her desk.

Rose lost... but so did Bridges. Rose knew they might need June Glume again, the best detective that ever served on the San Diego Police Department, even after she was disgraced and kicked to the curb like an empty forty-ounce malt liquor can on C Street. June cleared cases. June kicked ass. June was her hero... for a while.

CHAPTER 3

Ride share journal entry—June Glume

Driving enables me to remain sane… I can know people on the three terms of my choice, acknowledge, ignore, interact. I seldom interact.

The bimbo in the back is a millennial. I hate millennials… Not actual people in that age group, but the feckless turds who own the stereotype associated with the word millennial. Some of them are fine. But as a word of definition, millennial suggests a person who is a clueless, self-aggrandizing, and an all-around useless, lazy know-it-all. She was all that in spades.

The stripper shoes made her look taller than what I suspected her actual height to be… She had to be 5-1 on her best day otherwise, as skinny as a meth-head and wearing more make-up than a large clown. The micro-mini skirt and skimpy spaghetti strap top left nothing to the imagination, not that there was much up there to imagine.

Glancing in the rearview while bouncing over the ubiquitous San Diego potholes, I couldn't be certain, but it appeared that the tattoo on her neck that was supposed to say 'Serendipity' was misspelled, unless 'Serendripty' is a word. Classy.

Can women be cruelly critical to other women? Absolutely. But in this case, I am just reporting facts.

"I'm in a hurry… don't mess around." She blurted aggressively as she got in the back while video broadcasting herself on a popular social media platform du jour.

I said nothing… I decided 'not messing around' was in both our best interests.

She began loudly blathering on her phone to whoever was imprudent enough to watch her one-woman show. "Sorry… that was just the stupid ride-share driver. But at least I think she speaks English."

She laughed and laughed at her joke. I didn't laugh so much.

The girl rambled on to her audience, "And then I met this guy who was such a loser... I mean he was a complete loser... he shows up in khaki pants and an oxford... like... what are you, the help desk? I don't need any insurance. But I let him buy me an expensive dinner and drinks before I kicked his punk ass to the curb."

She began laughing so hard at her hilarious broadcast she almost lost it. She laid back and put her feet on the seat as only a skinny little fucker could do with a seat belt strapped and locked.

I involuntarily eye-rolled and she caught it in the mirror.

It lit her up.

"What's your problem, bitch?" she barked at me, clearly not considering the implications of her words.

"I need you to get your feet off the seat of my car... please." I said very politely.

In an act of insanity, she pushed her shoe up in my face. "Shut up and drive, asshole. Don't you know who I am?"

To her shock, the shoe in the face trick caused me to lose temporary control of my vehicle. At least that is the explanation I would add in the ride-share driver report later.

My car took a hard hop as I drove up on the sidewalk and jammed the brakes.

My passenger bounced around in the back seat like a tennis ball in a clothes dryer, ending ass up and sideways. "

"What in the fuck is wrong with you?" she cried out as she dropped her phone, confounding the hell out of her online fan base. After all, cool people like her don't get their ass kicked on social media.

I got out, opened the passenger door, unclicked her seatbelt, and dragged the rude little shit out of the car, her butt bouncing on the pavement as she skidded to the bus stop.

My internal car camera captured my being polite when she put her feet on the seat and her assaulting me with her feet. Those stiletto heels could put an eye out. I'd be fine if she filed a complaint. But now she was out of view of the ubiquitous big brother. Nobody else was around... so I snatched her phone out of her hand and turned it off. Then I politely explained something to her in the clearest terms possible as she sat on her pampered ass on the sidewalk.

"Listen, you rude little shitbird. You touch me again and I will beat your dumb ass senseless. If you ever disrespect another ride-share driver, I will find you and beat your dumb ass senseless. I have you on tape assaulting me so if I get any blowback from the company because of you, I'm filing charges. You are done. You'll never catch a ride-share again. I'll have someone dispatch a cab here to get your sorry ass, but you better grow up and recognize you are non-essential in the world of the living and breathing. Fuck you... and good day."

I thought saying 'good day' at the end was a pleasant touch. Professionalism is important in these situations.

I got back in my car, sent a cab to the bus stop, and then checked my interface... hmmm. business guy at the Hyatt heading for a restaurant in La Jolla... I punched the button on my phone and accepted the ride.

- End journal entry

Coronado, California

I finished writing the journal entry from my last ride-share passenger... I was still angry. Angry at her and angry at the world. It was time to get to the sand. Was my sanity gone? Or did I leave it at the beach? I'd look there first.

I caught myself muttering out loud like a schizophrenic street beggar.

Fuck the police department. Fuck Rose. Fuck the dead lady. Fuck the world...

More deep breaths.

I carried my beach chair, umbrella, and cooler full of pre-made cocktails down to the spit of sand at the end of D Avenue. It was warming up and boats of all descriptions cruised across the Big Bay, the sun flashing off their white hulls as they crossed the busy harbor.

I took one more deep breath... *Clear your head...*

It appeared that I had this stretch of sand to myself, or at least I believed so as I set up my chair, plopped down, and snatched the first pre-built cocktail out of the nylon cooler.

"June!" a hoarse, but sort of sexy voice called. It was the voice of someone who either yelled a lot, smoked for decades, or both.

Now what? I looked up to see one of my few local

acquaintances, Kimberly ambling over towards me from Centennial Park. Shit... I didn't want any company, although Kimberly Tyler is less annoying than most people.

Tyler, being a bit of a free spirit, plopped down in the sand beside my beach chair. "Why so Gloomy?" She wrinkled her mouth in a *'yeah, I said that shit'* grin, expecting either a single finger salute or laugh. Either would be fine with her.

I tried to smile, but I hated that joke... it wasn't funny in the first grade and it isn't funny now. But what are you going to do? Just be polite for a few minutes and she will leave.

But considering that most of my acquaintances are assholes, I have to admit that this lady is fairly interesting... former heavy metal roadie who now works with disabled kids, or at least she did until she retired two years ago. It doesn't suck to win the biggest lottery in ten years, purchase a big house on Coronado, and settle into a life of leisure. I'm not sure if she was a literal billionaire, but she had to be close.

I eyeballed her, wondering what it would be like to talk to someone I didn't particularly despise, for no purpose other than idle conversation. It might feel weird... but it might be worth a try. The shrink said to try and make a friend, which seemed like bullshit, but if you are going to have a friend, pick a wealthy one.

I gave it a shot. "Kimberly... long time no see. What's it been, a couple of months?" I asked, knowing it had been quite a while but forgetting actually how long it had been. A month? Three months? A year? Time gets messed up in my head.

Kimberly smiled graciously. "I know... it's been a while. I took a sabbatical. I've been in Ireland drinking in a pub with some mates... how about you? Staying busy?"

I thought before answering, still sizing up my visitor. That Ireland thing sounded like something Kimberly would do. I suspected she is a little older than me, maybe a bit wiser, and she definitely likes to be social... So, two good things out of three isn't bad. In an unprecedented act of restraint, I chose not to zap her with a stun gun. I continued this attempt at friend stuff a little longer. I wanted to see how it played out.

I elaborated on my immediate past, "Driving. Sleeping. Driving."

God, it's difficult talking this much... the art of conversation totally blows.

I summarized with, "That's about it."

Tyler smiled. My reply was brief, but it was still a reply.

I could read in her face what she was thinking. *At least June is trying*.

Tyler pressed on, "Fun... any good passenger stories?"

"No. Just the usual boring stuff. I forget them as soon as they get out of the car." I followed that statement with the exhausted sigh of a ditch digger. Pleasantness is exhausting.

"Oh." Kimberly sensed I was in no mood for a girl-time conversation, or perhaps she realized I was just shitty at it. She switched to the universal language of the weak and weary. "Say, I can run home and fetch a bottle of Crown Royal if you want. Today seems like a good 'beach drinks' day."

She had me at beach drinks, but I paused to think about it before responding. My chronically dark mood overrode my desire to be social. I wanted to say yes, but the words wouldn't form in my mouth. "Not in the mood, Kimberly. I need some time to think. Alone time."

I could tell Kimberly suspected she had stretched me beyond my limits at social life already. But she wouldn't quit. Not this close to a breakthrough. She was a social worker at heart. Or maybe she used to be a bartender.

"Think about what," Kimberly asked like a psychiatrist trying to trick repressed memories into revealing themselves.

I exhaled a long smoky breath that oozed out like a surrender… As much as I hated small talk, I really wanted to say it out loud. "The cops want my help."

It felt good, acknowledging out loud that the department might need me… even if it was simply as a murder witness.

"Wow... and you're thinking about it? After what they did to you?" Kimberly seemed skeptical.

I now knew I was locked in this conversation. The unspoken can of worms had just popped open, releasing a shit-ton of worm shit, bullshit, and other shit that I just didn't need to deal with right now.

Kimberly already heard my full story... all the ugly stuff that happened ending my police career.

What was it? A year ago when we talked last?

It was my own fault she knew about it. I let myself get drunk in public and let my guard down. In a near stupor, I opened up my bleeding little heart to chatty Kimberly during a Wednesday afternoon happy hour and spilled my guts. We had been serendipitously sitting side by side at the bar of the Little Tavern, a pub frequented by mostly locals, when it happened. I'm not sure what triggered my uncharacteristic girliness, but I chattered like a little ninth-grade whiny bitch... stupid tequila. Afterwards, though, Tyler wasn't a dick about my lengthy, seemingly endless soul cleansing burst of blathering, and I remembered how she demonstrated some highly refined listening skills during the drunken confession. She would have been a good interrogator, or therapist, or what are those things called... Oh yeah, a friend. I don't know why, but I couldn't make myself totally hate Kimberly's guts. Maybe because she was from far outside the justice system and she hated the government. Maybe because she wasn't a complete asshole. It could be her experience in the death metal music industry. Since that conversation, we maintained a passing 'Hi-Bye' relationship, which was an unusually deep bond for me.

I blinked once, pushing the reverie out of my mind... stupid PTSD... These mental shit strings seem so real. I hate drifting off so deeply into my mind in front of others. I refocused on the present.

I chose my words carefully, parsing them out in little chunks. "Yeah, they got a string of murders. For some reason, the cops think I might be of some assistance. But I passed on it, for now. Although..." I let the word linger in my ears... am I really saying this? I continued the thought, "I might look into the case on my own. I actually met the last victim a while back... a woman passenger... so... I'll think about it."

It was uncomfortable speaking those words yet somehow relieving to say them out loud. What kind of gypsy fortune teller crap is Kimberly pulling on me, I wondered? Did I just share something personal?

Tyler frowned. "Maybe, considering everything that happened, you should take a hard pass. It's not like the victim was someone you really knew. And you know the police brass will shit on you the first chance they get."

"I know, right? I didn't even like that snooty old bag. But... killers need to be brought before a judge or taken out on the street like the vicious animals they are. Maybe not by me..." I thought about the possibilities.

The addiction to being a cop is stronger than alcohol or drugs. I can't let it go.

Kimberly agreed, "Right. It's not your job."

I ignored her and continued, "even so, why not by me?" Something about the cold-blooded street murder of the nasty business broad was bothering me... but I couldn't put a finger on it. I decided I was in, but still not sure why or how.

Tyler was watching the wheels turning in my head, like she was trying to see what was happening inside my thick skull. She followed her instincts and jumped on board. "Okay, June. If you're really going to be a vigilante, I'll join you. This sounds like fun."

I gave her my best *'grin of contempt'* for the idea. "You don't want a part in this. You have too much to risk."

"And you don't?" Tyler asked.

"Not anymore. Being a burnout borderline alcoholic ride-share driver doesn't put me in the 'she's got so much to live for' category." I shared a rare smile, "And I like it that way."

"Then let's do this. You're working for me now, my personal detective on this case. I'll fund your investigation, but I want in on all the gory details. Being rich and having nothing to do sucks. I need this, June. I'll give you a thousand a week. Hell, I get a hell of a lot more than that every day on just my domestic investments. I'm bored... I'm missing out on life, stuck here driving expensive cars and drinking expensive booze and sleeping till noon every day. I want in. Come on, June. It's going to be fun."

Her comments on wealth and boredom caused me to involuntarily snort. I wasn't certain if it was a snort of humor or a snort of disgust. Like I mentioned, it was involuntary.

Kimberly pushed, "June... Let's do this!"

I needed the money and I half-assed trusted the skinny, long legged, mega-rich, blonde ex-rocker roadie. Besides, I have to have at least one person on the outside I can trust. Was it a risk? Yes, but when you got nothing, you aren't risking much.

What the hell.

"Deal," I said, as I reached into my cooler and retrieved one of my pre-built cocktails for Kimberly. "I guess I'm a 'personal detective' now. But I'm keeping my driving gig... just in case."

Kimberly laughed, "You got it, sister... Now let's celebrate."

After the first six cocktails, I realized I was hammered. I knew I was drunk because I couldn't get out of my beach chair without injuring myself... and I had an urgent need to wander down to the public restroom by the Ferry Landing... or was just walking home closer? I tried to calculate the distances in my alcohol induced haze. The math wasn't happening for me. I glanced over at my drinking companion. Tyler didn't seem fazed...

Must be those years working with rockers. They either live forever, or they die young, I mused. Tyler must have the Keith Richards/Willie Nelson music industry gene.

I watched as Tyler slugged down her last drink and bounced out of the chair with the energy of a teenager in a 1960s beach party movie. "I've had enough sun for the day. Here, let me help you up." She put out a hand.

"I don't need any help," I protested verbally, while gratefully accepting the help physically.

"Yeah, Kurt used to say shit like that."

I stood unsteadily. "Who?"

Kimberly folded my chair and zipped the cooler shut. "Some guitar player I used to know. He had a band. I worked for them in ninety-four until shit went south."

I was too drunk to comprehend the significance of that story, so I ignored her rock history lesson and unsteadily picked up my beach chair. "Yeah... so, meet here for sunset drinks?" I muttered... now warming up to the idea of working for a wealthy benefactor.

Some ideas really never make sense until you're drunk, I pontificated.

Best day ever.

San Diego PD - Homicide

Rose looked at the link analysis on the murders. There was something there. Some connection that she couldn't see. But it had to exist. These murders just didn't feel random. It felt like something more complex was going on. But what?

Murder number one was a month ago. A landscaper in North

Park found stabbed in an alley. Originally, a homicide supervisor classified it as a gang initiation, but that made little sense to her. She suspected that homicide was spray painting gang graffiti on their own scenes so they could dump the blame for not solving them on the task force or gang squad.

The gang squad called a 'bullshit' on the initiation theory too, but the brass kept the pressure on to keep the case declared as a gang thing since it happened on gang turf... or near gang turf. Plus, if gang murders go up, more federal anti-gang dollars get kicked into the city coffers. It's like getting paid to fail.

All that and gang initiation theory was the easiest path to making the case go away.

And all was good.

Until the second and third murders. The victims were a delivery driver and an investment banker. Body number four was a big-time realtor, and now five was the international businesswoman, a Columbian national. Different murder weapons, different MOs, but all within a brief period and with zero useful clues.

The victims seemed unrelated. Was this a serial killer murdering random people using a variety of MOs?

Rose knew it was something else. Now she had to convince her boss that something was wrong about this case, but she was stuck on the bottom of his shit list. It wasn't that long ago she could bounce ideas off June... she missed her. Rose sighed heavily. The truth was, she rode June's coattails most of her career. She might be reliable, but she didn't have the creative spark a detective like June had to sort out these whodunit cases. She'd be parked in juvenile or community relations doing dead-end crap if it wasn't for June. Rose needed a win on this case.

But for now, this investigation was going nowhere.

CHAPTER 4

Ride share journal entry—June Glume

Driving with a world-class hangover probably wasn't a good idea, but I needed to get off the island. Despite having a new job as a personal detective, whatever the hell that is, I still needed to drive. It can be an addiction. I don't know why. But I need to drive.

It was almost lunch when I hit the streets and made my way downtown. My first riders were a tourist couple from Florida in their mid-forties. They were chatty... They wanted to communicate with me, and when I say communicate, I mean they wanted to give me a non-stop narrative about how Florida is the superior place to live.

Don't get me wrong, I love Florida... but what I *don't* love is involuntarily suffering lectures inferring California's many shit-hole issues are *my fault*.

"We have sugar sand beaches."

"In Florida we have very clean cities," he added

"Florida doesn't get cold like this," she said smugly.

"The ocean is warm in Florida," he piped in again.

"Florida doesn't tax you like California," she stage-whispered disapprovingly. "We have better fishing in Florida too," she added, taking his turn to be a snobby-assed dick.

The woman couldn't shut up. He wasn't any better. I noticed she filled out her flowered muumuu like a bulky ham in cellophane, stretching its vast rolls of cotton to beyond the manufacturer's tolerance specifications, and he was a scrawny little mouse of a man sporting a Florida professional football team t-shirt that looked like it was four sizes too big for him. I almost forgot about pro-football since the local team stabbed the city in the back by leaving town. Soon after, the whole league went full commie... Now I was glad to see those pussies and their never-ending extortion racket go. There were a few good guys in the league to be sure, but the ninety percent who were assholes spoiled it for the rest of them.

I was taking the talkative couple from the Santa Fe Train Depot to the Hilton on the big bay when I noticed they were each holding one of those vaping thingies… I could tell that they wanted to vape in the car, but they were uncertain of the consequences, so they just held the devices nervously in their sweaty little Florida paws like a guy who is preparing to write a bad rent check holds a pen as the landlord looks on.

Having a new day job now, I felt comfortable being a bit of an asshole. I gave them fair but professional warning. "If either of you vape in my car, I'm dumping your asses on the street and letting the bums murder you."

The man apologized profusely. The hostile bums were standing on every corner and stretching out in every doorway of downtown, lingering around… looking dirty, smelly, and menacing. So this was a really effective threat. To someone who isn't used to it, downtown San Diego can look like the gates of hell. The two vaping devices quickly disappeared into pockets.

Any blowback from my harsh warning was not a concern. After a while, you a sense of who will take the extra effort to report you or give you a bad rating, and these two clowns weren't going to do anything. A secondary benefit of my assholery was that they both shut their yaps for the rest of the trip.

I dumped them out under the massive overhang in front of their hotel. I drove back on Park Boulevard and down Marina Park Way to get a burger and a beer at the bait shop diner near the fishing pier… Best in San Diego, in my expert opinion. This painful ride had cured my jones for driving. It was time to have a cold one and get to work on the murder.

-end journal entry

Burger Stand

Ernie Samuels was working the counter. It wasn't much of a counter, four metal stools… the rest of the seating was picnic tables off to the side. The beefy old Irishman shoved his freckled kisser in my face. "Glume, you'll never guess who was here this morning campaigning."

He was right, I would never guess. Because I don't give a shit. But I played along anyway since I needed my food, and he hadn't brought it to me yet. I shrugged.

He whispered to me now, using the tenor of an underworld informant spilling information to a G-Man under a foggy lamp post in 1930s Chicago. "That rat bastard Costa… Councilman Costa. He says he wants to be a state representative but I think the SOB wants to be president… or king. I tell you that bastard is delusional."

Costa's political aspirations did not impress me. He humiliated me on live television at a council meeting, or at least he had tried to. I had just gotten an award for nabbing a serial killer when the dickless wonder called me back up to the front of the council and began chastising me for arresting him four years earlier.

The cameras were still rolling. I could sense the local news media turds getting excited.

He called me a racist and a jack-booted thug. I just smiled and walked away. It wasn't a fight that I was going to win, and to be honest, I just didn't care what this turd said.

Oh yeah, some of what he said was true. I *did* arrest his worthless ass four years before that little performance in Council Chambers. It happened back when he was a just a piece of shit community activist, which is French for full-time-communist-dickhead. He stuck his nose in my business while I was trying to do CPR on a heart attack victim, shoving a phone camera in my face and accusing me of being part of an institutionally racist police department… he chattered something about the victim being white and me being white and if it was a minority having a heart attack, I wouldn't have taken life-saving measures. His rant was distracting… and he kept getting in my way. Naturally, I cuffed his ass up and left him face down on the sidewalk until Fire arrived and took over my victim's care. I booked his dumb ass, but a week later, the DA dropped charges since Costa claimed he was providing a voice for his underserved community and was exercising free speech. The DA was a pussy and a democrat. The puke walked. Typical bullshit that happens in most of America's big cities now, I guess.

A year and a half later, he became a councilman in a mainly Hispanic neighborhood. The voters thought he was Hispanic. He never said otherwise. In fact, he did everything he could to let them believe he was Hispanic. I did some digging and found out his dad was of Italian descent. He sold used cars in Pomona. The old man really played up his Italian ancestry. He called himself the Roman Gladiator of Used Cars on cheesy TV commercials. He even had a cool Roman soldier outfit. His mom's maiden name was Silverstein… She was from Queens, but her sister married a Puerto Rican dude, so he claimed he was from a Hispanic family based on his uncle-in-law's heritage and thus managed to portray himself a Hispanic civil rights activist. He looked more like a fat Liza Minnelli with a mustache than he did a Latino. Unfortunately, the impoverished Hispanic voters living in the district bought the scam or sold their ballots.

Did I mention he was the loudest voice supporting my termination from the police department?

I asked my burger guy the next logical question. "So, did you give him money, Ernie?"

Samuels looked sheepish. "Yeah, I gave the little worm fifty bucks… just to get his ass out of here. He could rezone me right out of business if he wanted to. I don't have a choice with these parasites."

I snorted in disgust. "I don't blame you. These politicians bleed local businesses for every dime they can get, the entitled pricks." I was hoping the display of enthusiastic sympathy would get me a discount on the meal. I send a lot of tourists his way and I remind him of it at every opportunity.

Another mug sat down and ordered some food, ending our conversation. A few minutes later, Ernie showed up with my burger. I decided to ask him a question while I had a chance. "So, what is Costa's pitch?"

"He's into this marijuana dispensary issue now. To tell you the truth, I don't know if he's for it or against it, but that's his thing. I don't follow local politics much. I try to just pay him the shakedown money and tune his ass out."

I quit talking and focused on my burger. Delicious… it had a thick slice of tomato, crisp lettuce, spicy mustard, some steak sauce, American cheese, and a bunch of thick pickle slices, and not just generic pickles but good ones that packed a bite and had some crunch to their texture. Delicious. The French fries were to die for. They were basically a couple of potatoes cut in half and deep fried.

I went into a lucid trance as I dug in… my mind wandered in an out-of-body state of being. *You are doing God's work, Ernie… this is what potatoes were meant for… this and vodka… and potato salad,* I thought.

I finished my meal and tried to push a twenty his way. He pushed it back. "Not this time June Bug. I appreciate you sending the business this way. This time it's on me."

Ernie Samuels was one of the few humans I allowed to call me June Bug. My mom called me that when I was a kid. That was okay. But after I joined the military, I figured I better get some respect and not allow others to pull that familiar-assed shit on me. But Big Ernie and his diminutive red-headed, freckled wife Betty and their nine red-headed freckled kids could call me June Bug. Mainly because when the kids were working, they called me Aunt June Bug and gave me extra pickles and extra fries. I don't know why they like me. Maybe because of that time a stoned-out park bum tried to rob Betty at knife point and I karate chopped that fucker in the throat. Or maybe they just like me because I'm so pleasant to be around.

I chugged my beer and left. It was time to find the killer.

The Big Picture Coffee Shop—6th Avenue, Downtown San Diego

I made the call and waited at the table outside for my ex-partner. The little hole-in-the-wall coffee shop had the best coffee in the Gaslamp Quarter. The owner allowed local artists to display their work. Numerous paintings by aspiring artists adorned the walls. Most of them sucked, but I'm no art critic. I was fine with dogs playing poker on velvet. I still have a velvet Elvis painting from TJ hanging in my spare bedroom.

A few minutes later, I spotted dumb ass Rose parking her city car across the street. She popped a quarter into the meter. *Why in the hell should a cop pay to park a city car on a city street,* I thought… *pussies.* Downtown a quarter will only buy you ten or fifteen minutes anyway.

Rose was wearing her sensible masculine mailman shoes and looked as unfeminine as a woman could look. I was used to it. I'd be shocked if she ever allowed herself to look good at work. She's that way. I don't know why.

"June… I'm surprised you called. I've missed you." Rose said sincerely.

Rose always speaks from the heart… which is odd for a detective. But I didn't care about sincerity. I had something on my mind, so I got directly to the point. "Look Rose, I want to know everything you have on the murder and any related murders. Is there a ride-share serial killer?"

"So, you didn't miss me? You're not here to apologize for being mean?" Rose asked, more than a little butt hurt and ignoring my question.

I could tell she was butt hurt by her lower lip hanging like a sad little baby.

"Rose, you called me first. If it helps, I'm sorry I wished you were dead. That was wrong. In fact, I'm glad you're alive. You can give me information if you're alive."

Rose didn't seem to swoon over my very heartfelt apology.

"Fuck you, June… You are worse than ever. What the hell is wrong with you…" then she paused, "wait… are you interested in the case?"

"Maybe… yeah, I might have some interest."

She went from sad to anxious. "Do you know something? Did you remember something?"

Rose might be a bit of a whiner, but she's still one hundred percent cop, a total blue blood.

I played my cards close to the vest… if I had cards… and if I had a vest… It's a figure of speech. I went with a densely shielded honest answer. "I have a client."

"Come on, June. You don't have a PI license." Rose instinctively called out every violation of the law that came to her attention.

"I'm getting one."

"When?" she asked, like it mattered.

I could see an expression of disbelief mixed with hope wrinkling up the features on her face. "Real soon, Rose," I lied. "Now what do you have?"

Rose pulled out a folder. A piece of paper inside had a little diagram. It was neatly drawn in various-colored ink and in careful detail. "We have some murders. I think they're related. But I'm not sure how."

"I thought this was some kind of ride-share case?" I asked.

"We all did until somebody pointed at that ride-share is so

ubiquitous that it somehow ties into almost every assault, disturbing the peace, trespassing, and burglary too.... It was a phony baloney statistic. Ninety percent of all crimes have a ride-share component. But you know as well as I do that crime statistics are bullshit, so... there's that."

Crime Analysts, polygraph operators, and behavioral profilers are the gypsy fortune tellers of law enforcement. They know jack-shit about crime, but the brass always relies on them as a political crutch. In their defense, they have excellent hind-sight.

"So, what's this chart?" I asked. It was too pretty. It looked like it belonged in a craft store instead of a squad room. I felt compelled to sit my coffee cup on it and give it a nice round circular stain. But I didn't. Rose would shit.

"This is an outline of murders... all unsolved, no clear relationship to one another, but something is going on. They all occurred in the greater downtown area. All were violent deaths... gun, knife, blunt instrument, strangulation."

"That's it?" I wasn't seeing much of a relationship.

"It's the absence of data, June. Look at this. Murders have clues. A partner, a friend, a lover, a witness. These deaths are geographically connected to downtown and none of them have one iota of actionable evidence."

"Can I have a copy of this shit?" I asked, maybe a bit too aggressively.

"Hell no!... You aren't a cop anymore. Bridges told me to treat you like a snitch... I'm trying to be respectful Juney... What the hell is wrong with you?"

Why do people always ask what the hell is wrong with me? It should be obvious.

I took a deep breath. Maybe I needed a pill. I'm being an asshole. I know it. But I can't help it. The city screwed me. I hate them all. But... I don't hate Rose. We were friends in patrol before we were detectives and working patrol is a connection that lasts as long as we both breathe. Because even if you hate each other's guts, when you work patrol together, you have a special bond.

I responded by trying to use my sincere voice. "You're right. I'm sorry Rose. Is there a way I can do more? I want to help you, not Bridges. Just you."

Rose put her hand on mine in a sisterly way. It felt weird; I had a sensation of warmth coursing through the top of my head. The intrusive move did not offend me and I didn't jerk away, which was odd for me.

"June, I'll give you what I got. But I need to know what you remember about the lady in your ride-share. She was the gunshot victim… please… help me."

I gave it up. "Fine. I'll write out a statement and email it to you. I'll sign it later. Will that work?"

Rose bestowed one of her saintly smiles of forgiveness and redemption upon me. It was sort of annoying. But I sort of liked it… a little.

She continued, "That would help a lot. And here." She reached in her folio and pulled out a yellow eight by eleven envelope. "This is for you. It's everything I got. Don't get caught with it."

"You got it Rose." I was surprised but grateful. I forced myself to be nice… it hurt… but I gave it my best shot. "Seriously, thank you, Rose. I appreciate this. We'll get that scumbag. I promise you."

Rose patted my hand like an approving grandma, got up, and wandered back towards her car. She stopped in the middle of 6th Avenue and looked back. My wistful-eyed ex-partner began to speak, but didn't. She turned and ran.

Why?

Then I realized she spotted a parking meter wagon rolling up on her quickly. Rose hopped into her city car and sped off. Is that what criminal justice has come to? Meter enforcement employees are trying to nail homicide detectives? This city is doomed. Fucking people.

I finished my coffee while I did a quick read of the file. It was pretty clear that some shit had gone down in the streets of San Diego. Nasty shit. Dead guys. Clever killers. This was going to be fun.

Coronado, California

I cruised through Barrio Logan and hopped on the 75 ramp to the massive bridge separating downtown stank from the refreshing sea air of paradise. There wasn't any traffic heading into Coronado, so I could safely take in the view of the Pacific as I crested the top of the span. Arriving home, I dialed Kimberly to tell her about the

traction I was getting on the case. She was my boss now…
unofficially. I like to keep the boss up to speed. She answered on the
first ring, and I gave her the briefing.

"Kimberly. I got a file from the police. Looks like we're in
business. Speaking of, if you are serious about this, I need to file for
a private investigator license. One of the detectives called me out on
it today."

Kimberly answered, sounding like she was suppressing a
giggle. "No worries, mate. I have one. You can work under my
license."

"What? That's impossible. You have to have experience and
background checks to get a PI ticket… there's a bunch of drama
involved in getting these licenses."

"No… well, *maybe* there is. But I called Gavin and made a
$25,000 dollar donation to his campaign and he got me one this
afternoon. Don't you know how Sacramento works, honey? It's all
about the money."

Then I heard her growl out an imitation of an electric guitar riff
from the Beatle's version of the old rhythm and blues tune *Money,
that's what I want*… I could picture her dancing around playing air
guitar… I didn't need to ask, I just knew.

"Really?" I exaggerated my speech as my skepticism abounds.

"Seriously, June. They do this all the time. I never knew until I
had serious cash. After I won the lottery, Gavin called me up asking
for a donation. I thought it was friends pulling a gag, so I said sure,
I'll give you ten thousand for a state realtor license and the next day
I had one. It's hilarious. They offered me a position on the Coastal
Commission for a million bucks. I told them to blow me, but I'd be
in touch if things changed. It's a total criminal syndicate up there,
June. I love it."

"Gavin?" I asked, a little surprised she would know someone
that high in government… or that he would call her… how would
he know her number? Oh… lottery commission… makes sense.

"Yeah, the little worm… He's such a pussy." Kimberly
snickered.

"So… I'm your employee officially?"

"Yep, I had my attorney do attorney stuff and we now have an
office in downtown Coronado with you listed as my PI employee. I
call it Death Metal Investigations… because it sounds bad ass…

what do you think?"

"Kimberly, I could lick your face right now." Now I was giddy too and feeling a little sassy. Knowing rich people is fun. I had no idea.

She giggled, "As enticing as that sounds, let's just get to work tomorrow at… what time is it that detectives call nine o'clock?"

"We call it nine o'clock."

"I thought it was something hundred hours?"

"We don't say that shit unless we need to sound all tactical in front of the public."

"Cool… see you then." She gave me the address of the office and disconnected.

This was splendid news. Something to be excited about again… but I'm not giving up my ride share gig. It's my lifeline, the safe space.

CHAPTER 5

Ride share journal entry—June Glume

Some riders you never forget. Some you forget immediately. I had the latter in the car most of the day until later in the afternoon when I picked up some French guy. He might have been the prettiest man I had ever seen. His dark blue suit was impeccable. He had a fine manicure with nail polish. He was handsome as a movie star but still exuded manliness... in my old line of work, especially with the comic book convention in San Diego every year, I met my share of action movie stars and most of them were pussies... not Chuck of course, but most of the other ones. This guy was polite and a bit chatty. He told me he was an engineer from Yema watches. I wear the same old G-Shock I wore on the PD, so I wouldn't know a Yema watch from Big Ben. But I concluded immediately that I needed a Yema watch. I dropped him off at the Symphony Towers and lingered at the curb long enough to watch him walk in.

I think I need to find a man too.

- End journal entry

Coronado, California - Death Metal Investigations Business Office

Each index card in my pocket had a dead guy's information written out. I didn't want to get caught on the street with a police file. For now, this was good enough to get started. I was ready to launch my investigation. But first I had to swing by the shop and check in with Kimberly. I realized I was looking forward to seeing the place. It had been a long time since I'd looked forward to anything. A tsunami of negative shit roiling over the sandy beach of your life will do that to you.

I found a parking spot without a meter on Adella Avenue and

peacefully strolled by the beautiful homes on my pleasant two-block walk to the office. For all the time I had been on Coronado, I had never actually been above the ground floor of this office building. The offices were in the three stories above the ground floor retail shops, which is the height limit for the town, and the top floor had some keen ocean views. It was also close to many local establishments hosting happy hour, so things were looking good.

I climbed the outside stairway to the office and knocked on the door bearing the suite number she gave me… 221. It was inconsistent with the rest of the building's numbering system. What the hell?

Kimberly shouted from inside, "Glume, get your ass in here."

Already barking orders, and she'd been my boss now for one second. But to be honest, it was more of a 'you got to *see* this shit' order rather than a 'get your ass in gear and *do* this shit' order.

I let myself in. There was a small reception area and three offices, all with views of downtown Coronado. In the center office, I saw Kimberly sitting behind a desk, talking to a long-haired dude. Her black cat was sleeping on the bookcase behind her.

"June… meet Dee. He's with his wife, kids, and grandkids over at the Del taking a brief vacation. We just had coffee and I'm showing him the place."

He stood up, and I shook his hand. Dee looked like a typical vacationer except for the long hair and jewelry. He was about mid-sixties, lean and tan. Definitely a man of some means.

I mustered some courtesy. It was painful, but when you are a businessperson, you have to put up with being congenial once in a while, even if you hate almost everyone. "Nice to meet you, Dee. I'm June."

We shook hands. He responded.

"My pleasure, June…" he looked me over, apparently eyeballing my black jeans, black t-shirt, SWAT boots, and black leather blazer. "Goth?"

"No… classical American badass."

"Cool."

I could hear some New Yorker in his voice. He was polite, but we all stood there awkwardly, like we expected something should happen, but it didn't. I suddenly realized that he is famous. Every time I've ever met someone famous, there is always an awkward pause while they wait for you to ask them for something, a photo, autograph, a loan... I experienced a slight wave of embarrassment come over me because I did not know who he was, other than a standard-issue pretentious knob. Kimberly interceded.

"Dee is a singer," Kimberly said flatly, like I should know that.

That description made him snicker.

I didn't snicker... I didn't even give a shit. I hate celebrities. Except Chuck, of course. The lone wolf doesn't care if you recognize him. He recognizes you.

I continued with the polite thing. "Nice. I'll try to listen to one of your songs on the radio."

"We're not going to take it?" He inquired.

Odd thing to ask, I thought.

"Take what?" I asked.

They both laughed at my question.

I'm not a big fan of these two right now.

Kimberly raised her hand to hide her mouth, and stage whispered toward his ear. "Dee, she isn't into the same music as us," she explained with the smile of someone telling an inside joke. Kimberly turned her attention back to me and started talking like the teacher she used to be as a pre-lottery jackpot winner. "June, he has been a world class singer for decades, adored by millions as a music industry icon, a rock-and-roll icon, he is... iconic."

Well, I love music, but I don't pay attention to the names of the bands much. And Kimberly was getting weird on her hero worship reverence about this skinny creep. I rejoined the conversation, now fully informed of Dee's music royalty. "Nice. I'm happy for you, Dee. I was a cop. Millions of people hate me in an iconic way, so we have that in common. Iconic."

For some reason, that comment cracked him up.

Dee put his hand up for a high-five. I returned the gesture. I don't care if he is a dick. I'm not leaving him hanging. He's Kim's friend and I'm not her mom.

He responded, "Well, June... as one icon to another, you have your hands full working with Kimberly." Dee continued talking to me while turning to look at Kimberly. "I could tell stories..." His voice trailed off.

Kimberly interrupted, "But he won't." She playfully bum-rushed him out the door.

"I wanna rock! Platinum, June... Platinum!" He laughed as he waved goodbye.

Whatever the hell that means... I faked a pleasantry that I didn't mean. "Nice meeting you." He might be Kimberly's friend, but wow, such a totally obnoxious dick. His self-awareness level was about zero.

I followed Kimberly and Dee out the door. Pausing at the railing, I lit a cigarette on the deck as they giggled their way down the stairs. Smoking was illegal in Coronado, but I am not convinced that stupid regulation applied to me. They let hippies smoke pot, hipsters vape clouds of candy flavored steam, and sailors smoke cigars, but somehow Coronado decided cigarettes are verboten. I think our town council is one of the many government organizations taking orders from the CCP, who curiously, let their guys smoke. Commies.

Kimberly interrupted my deep thoughts on local politics when she returned one cigarette later, after walking her friend back to Orange Avenue. *Shit*, now *she* was vaping. I hate stinky hipster perfume smell. Well, she writes the paychecks... and she's close to achieving billionaire status, so... Vape away pal, vape away. I have no fucks to give about it.

"Want to see your office?" she asked.

"Office?"

The announcement that I had an office surprised me. For some reason, I didn't think I'd have an office. At the police department, I was just an asshole at a desk in a room full of other assholes at desks. That's why I always tried to stay on the street.

"Sure... let's see it. Let me finish this smoke."

We stood on the deck, her vaping and me smoking, both of us generally fucking up the atmosphere. A middle-aged lady on the sidewalk lumbered by carrying some parcel from the post office next door, sporting her *'I want to see the manager'* haircut. She sniffed in the air like a hound dog a couple of times before yelling up at us, "You can't smoke here. It's illegal. I'm calling the cops."

I gave her a hard look. She was wearing a blue V-neck tee-shirt with glitter glued to it, white capri pants, and flip-flops. She had a huge butt and was flatter than a rotary club speech. I'd seen her busy body kind before.

I started to flip my cigarette butt at her, but Kimberly stopped me. She gave the old crank a pleasant smile and apologized. "We'll put them out... so sorry. We're from Imperial Beach, we didn't know."

The old lady scowled and marched off, satisfied that the lowly Imperial Beach residents wouldn't know any better.

Snobby old bag. I like Imperial Beach.

I finished my smoke... there were maybe one-point-four puffs left on it. *It's not like I'm addicted to smoking. I can quit if I want to. At least I'm not vaping.*

I ran out of lies to tell myself.

Screw it.

I took one more hard drag before launching it at the busybody old lady's wake.

Kimberly led us into the office suite and pointed to the one on the left. "All yours, June."

Wow, it was nice. Nicer than I expected. I had a mission style wooden desk, an antique desk lamp, and... an ashtray... I almost cried. I miss ash trays... I miss them so very much.

I had a gigantic window with a view of a parking garage. I'd take it. This was better than I was used to having... but all this gleeful ambiance was making me uncomfortable. Good never comes unless it brings its old friend bad with it. I needed to get in the car and get some ride-shares... coffee, ephedrine, the street... I needed it. I suddenly felt a twinge of resentment for Kimberly changing up my life. I liked my life. This lifestyle isn't me... I need a drink... I need the street.

Then I felt Kimberly grab my arm... I jerked away without thinking.

"Where were you, June?" Her face was drawn in concern.

"What?" I forgot where I was.... Stupid.

Kimberly patiently asked again, "Where were you? You like... zoned out."

"No, I didn't." When in doubt, hostility and denial are my default modes.

She gently pressed the issue. "Yes, you did... for almost a minute... What's up?"

"I don't know..." I changed the subject. "I have some stuff on the case... do you want to hear it?"

I tried to shine her on. The hard truth is, I don't want my little addictions and PTSD to screw up this new gig. Even though I might deny that information to Kimberly, I needed it. My psyche just wasn't up to the acute transition. I'd been out of the world for too long. I don't think it wanted me back.

Kimberly didn't make an issue out of my display of a clench jawed thousand-yard stare. She's good. I wondered where she learned how to handle stressed out psychos. Maybe she was an ex-bartender. She managed me like a professional, almost like a cop handles a crime victim. Maybe not all cops, but the old ones who have seen too much. The kind of cops who drag a heavy canvas bag of guilt and failure behind them every day of their life because no matter what they tried to do to make things better, the world is still a shithole of misery and suffering. And even if you win one and send some maggot to the joint or county hospital, or the morgue, your victims have already lost before that game even began. Detectives know… they feel the weight. Detectives who were like me when I was a real cop and wasn't a drug-abusing border-line psychopath. Long ago… When I was happy.

She asked again, interrupting my pity party. "Yeah… what's up with the case? That's why we're here."

I let my bout of recurring depression slip out. "I might have been out too long. I'm not sure I'm good at this anymore."

"Being a cop?"

"Yeah."

"What do you do for a living now, Glume? Besides this."

"Ride share… you know that."

"So, you drive around the city, find strangers, stuff them in the back of your car and haul them off. Aside from the jail part, how is that different from what cops do?"

I hate her. She almost made me snicker.

"I uh…"

"Glume, we can do this!"

I thought about it… tried to focus… I recalled what it felt like getting hired, being an academy graduate… I had been in the Army, so I was in shape and tough… the academy was easy for me, but I didn't have friends. I never have friends… Do I have a friend now?

Shit, I was already zoning again. I continued. "I talked to a former friend in homicide."

Kimberly asked, "Former? Man or woman?"

I thought that was an interesting clarification request. Maybe rockers think differently than cops. That could be helpful. I clarified. "A woman… her name is Rose. She's good. A bit of a doormat, but good at her job."

"What did your former friend say?"

Wow… Kimberly is really getting into this detective supervisor thing. Funny, she's better than some of them I worked with at

SDPD. I guess being a roadie for a metal band is good experience for supervising rogue detectives and fucked up cases.

"She told me that shit is seriously fucked up at San Diego PD homicide. They have bodies stacking up. Maybe a serial killer, but not the usual kind. No clear relationships in the victims' backgrounds other than getting whacked in a variety of messy ways and having the audacity to die in the streets of America's greatest city."

"Hey, it's better than fucking Baltimore." she countered, defending our big city across the bay.

"So is an infected hemorrhoid," I argued.

"Point taken." Her lips pinched up like she was going to either pout or spit. "So, what is next?"

"I have to develop a lead."

"How are you going to do that?"

I looked at her before speaking. Is she using the Socratic method on me? Maybe there is more to this girl than rock-and-roll and mega-bucks.

"I'm going to drive. You can't break a case sitting in a cubical with a computer. You have to be on the street. I'm going to do some ride-share… It helps me get my head straight… maybe revisit the crime scenes and knock on doors… see what there is to see. Drink a bunch of coffee. Smoke some cigarettes. It's called shoe leather detective work, Kimberly. It's what separates a real detective from a generic knob in a suit carrying a notebook and a gun. I'll keep you posted."

Kimberly gave me a funny look. Not ha-ha funny, and not condescending… just that she was seeing a side of me or maybe a side of detective work that she hadn't considered before. Shit… she might learn this trade after all. She's a smart girl… maybe too smart.

I walked down the stairs to the street, grabbed a strong black coffee at the franchise bagel shop on Orange Avenue, found a chair and table outside, and went to work. I wanted to make sure I was up to speed before I crossed the bridge.

My first order of business was to call Rose. There might be something missing.

"Detective Lopez."

"Rose, Glume. Did the murder victim at the Embarcadero, the Columbian woman… did she have a briefcase?"

"Let me look."

I sipped some of my dark roast while I waited.

"June, she had a leather briefcase."

"Were there documents in it?"

"I don't know. I can't find the inventory of the contents. It's not with my file."

"Try to find it."

I disconnected before she asked me how I have been. She loves small talk. Small talk makes me want to puke.

But if I am the only witness we have who had any prior contact with this mystery woman, I needed to recall everything about her ride. I flipped through my journal. Not much there, but I remember her reading a letter or document of some kind and seeming significantly concerned about it. Maybe it was something. Concentrating on that day, I tried to remember more. My photographic memory is a nightmare condition I must medicate with drugs and alcohol. But on the job, this particular curse can come in handy. I remembered the woman's face; she seemed worried. I recalled everything about her clothes and style. She was a sophisticated woman. But there was something else I was still missing. Oh yeah, she signed the document. The woman used a Meisterstück Solitaire Blue Hour LeGrand Fountain Pen by Mont Blanc. I know everything there is to know about that luxury brand. I recovered a hundred-thousand bucks worth of counterfeit ones in Imperial Beach when I was working burglary as a rookie detective.

She was left-handed. She signed something. Her signature? An approval? I gleaned much of my recollection from quick glances in the rear-view and my peripheral vision, but I was sure of it. She scribbled something on the document.

What did our dead mystery woman sign?

Was it important?

Meaningless?

Maybe.

Maybe if I hit the street for a while, I'd figure it out.

I needed to get my ride-share fix in.

Ride share journal entry – June Glume

I no sooner crossed the bridge back into San Diego when I got a request to pick someone up near the Iris Transit Station in the East Village. It was an older lady... not old-old, but maybe about mid-fifties.

I popped some diet pills I had, washed them down with a sip of another black coffee, touched the icon on my phone accepting the ride gig, and headed for the pickup point.

I saw the couple from a block away. A man was trying to protect the woman behind him. They looked like an older married tourist couple. He was shielding her from some crazy street bum haranguing them... The bum waved his arms wildly, yelling and circling them like a jackal, a six-foot-six smelly, dirty jackal. They were trying hard to psychically teleport themselves to anywhere but the transit station area. I could see another half a dozen miscellaneous hobos down the block further yelling, too. They were just too lazy to pursue the couple as far as the mega-bum did. They had no work ethic.

I had my window down and could hear the standard downtown street bum rants... "God wants you dead... you can't wear gray here. I'm the devil... I am the voice of the lord..." The bum was screaming rapid-fire, incoherent bum-babble in the poor man's face.

The bum had the scam down perfectly. The old *'waving my arms threateningly in your face like I might hit you, but if you strike me in self-defense, I'll call it assault and sue you'* move. Unfortunately, the local commie DA would prosecute it, probably call it a hate crime, and send the old man to prison if he so much as touched one of the city's precious street bums.

There wasn't enough assholery occurring at this point for me to smoke the prick with my Glock. Fortunately, I keep a ball bat and ball glove in the car with me; I don't play softball and the glove is just a cover to re-classify my bat from 'malicious blunt instrument' status to 'random sporting equipment on hand' status.

I rolled up and got out of the car with my pink aluminum ball bat. "Scram, maggot, before I find out if I can home-run-derby your fat melon head into Petco Park from here."

The bum was cautiously defiant. "Nobody says scram anymore. It ain't cool."

That was a counterargument I had not expected.

I still say scram and I'm cool.

Fuck this guy.

"Fine, I'm knocking your damned head off just for shits and giggles then, asshole." I did a little baton twirl with the bat like it was a ninja sword and then assumed a more traditional American batting stance, somewhat like the immortal Ted Williams, a local favorite, and historic bad ass.

The look on the bum's face told me he was suddenly in tune with the universe. Crazy or not, he knew I was serious, so he made what might have been his first wise choice in the past twenty years. He burned a direct and expedient path towards the blue line train, swearing and swinging his arms around like a malevolent windmill, but not making eye contact with us.

Fucker.

I lowered the bat and relaxed… at least as much as I am capable of relaxing behind enemy lines.

The lady hugged me.

"Thank you," she blurted… "Oh my god… we got lost… we thought we could take a trolley and these… these… these people started surrounding us and wouldn't let us alone."

The man shook my hand. "I have a bad heart… I wouldn't last a minute in a fight… thank you."

He was maybe seventy… she was clearly a decade or so older than the photo she used on the app… after a while, everyone uses a younger photo of themselves… I don't know why. I'll find out when I get older, I guess.

When she finally finished hugging me and he finished shaking my hand, I opened the back door of my car for them.

"All part of the service… hop in and I'll take you back to the Marriott. But from now on, *do not* use public transportation and *do not* walk past 6th Avenue…. the area beyond that is for trained locals only… well, maybe trained locals and the dumb ass hipsters who walk among the bums staring into their phones like zombies. They're expendable though."

The lady's eyes widened. "Oh, my… I had no idea… what's a hipster?"

"Do you know what a beatnik is?"

"Yes."

"A hipster is the unholy spawn of beatniks and communists."

"So, assholes?" the man asked.

I ignored his question and continued my lecture. "City Hall pulled the cops off the job here. This is a no-man's-land. They beat a guy to death over by the pedestrian overpass not long ago." I pointed to the bridge that connected a massive bayside hotel to the ballpark.

Glancing nervously about, they hopped into the back seat like it my car was the last helicopter out of Saigon. I got a fifty-dollar cash tip and another hardy handshake when I dropped them off in a safer location in Little Italy.

- End journal entry

Downtown San Diego—Gaslamp Quarter

I used some of my fifty buck tip to buy some more over-the-counter stay-awake pills. The drugs were kicking in and I felt that warm buzz of intensity, reducing my PTSD depression to a dark whisper in the wind.

Compulsive tendencies… cranking up a couple of notches. Hypervigilance operating at a 'first-day-in-prison level.' I could feel my heart race. Oh yeah.

Balance… must try to balance.

I need to Irish up my coffee. That should do the trick.

Yanking the wheel hard right, I hopped up over the curb in front of a pub on 4th Avenue between Market and Island. They open early.

Hmmm… only one wheel on the sidewalk… meh… it'll be fine.

I didn't have to say anything. I just stood at the bar and held the cup out at arm's length and my head down. Maggie, the day shift bartender, quickly splashed some Jack into a shot glass and then dumped it in my cardboard container of delicious black caffeine. She repeated it once more, then stared at me in anticipation.

I mumbled, or shouted, or simply spoke… not sure how I got the words out… "We're good."

The blonde bartender smiled widely. "Good morning, Junie… Kill anybody yet today?"

Maggie didn't have a lot of friends who have killed people, so she really loved that about me. I didn't care. I killed for the job on the PD, and I killed in the army… all good… it's just killing, not murdering… a little white lie that allows me to sleep at night, sort of… with the assistance of illegal medication, cough syrup, and booze.

I took a sip before answering. "It's still early, baby…"

Maggie is gay. She loves it when I flirt with her. I love it when she provides free whiskey supplements for my coffee… it's a match made in heaven.

Does that make me a whore?

I'm not gay… she knows it. But I think she really believes that she can persuade me to switch teams.

She pouted a suggestive pass. "Come in some night, June… we can hang. I promise it will be fun."

This girl exudes sexiness. She's five-three, built like the proverbial brick shit house, and has long soft blonde hair draped over her shoulders, making her steel-blue eyes glimmer. And that cute little waitress uniform… Wait. What am I saying? Are her charms are working on me?

Deep breath.

No thanks. I'm wired to prefer guys, but if I ever *did* switch teams, I'd call her first.

I kept it professional. "Got to work, Mag… Living the good life isn't cheap on the coast."

She gave me a longing gaze. "I could make life really fantastic, June."

I changed the subject. "What's up with all these people getting whacked around town lately?" Maggie was a good bartender, but it was easy to get her off the flirting track and onto the informant track without her knowing she was an informant.

Yeah… I use my friends. I'm an asshole.

"I heard gangs, I heard serial killer, I even heard some asshole insisting it was marijuana. Some old guy... maybe thirty-five... I think he was a business guy... he was weird though."

"Nobody kills someone on a pot deal, do they?"

It just didn't sound right unless we were talking real weight... but I'm old school. Most of the victims didn't have the money to do weight... so a murder spree over an ounce? Not likely.

Mag editorialized the downtown situation. "People are starting to kill people for no reason at all around here. They killed a night manager on 5th Avenue a week ago. I think the cops quit beating up hoodlums because the mayor is a pussy and now the hoods run downtown. Shakedowns, robberies, assaults... It's not safe anymore. I'm glad I work the day shift."

She didn't know shit that wasn't already in the newspapers and her 'old guy' was probably some tourist who didn't know shit, just hitting on her. Marijuana was a stupid motive. Her old guy source was probably a software developer from Pittsburg or some shit. Although it is funny that he thought he had a shot with her.

It was time to go.

"I have to jet, Maggie. Thanks for the refreshment." I winked and made a kiss noise.

"Come back soon, June Glume." She giggled at her near rhyme. It was nice to hear. It's rare that anyone wants me to come back soon. At least people who know me.

The coffee and Jack elixir was working... the dope and the enhanced brew were leveling me out. I could begin to see clearly and think clearly... not my favorite condition, but there was work to do.

I got out to my car, went around the block navigating a maze of one-way streets and construction, then drove in the other direction up Banker's Hill to Balboa Park. There was a place open where I could park in the shade, so I stopped, rolled down the windows, and sucked in the calm... It was time to find some crime scenes. I pulled the note cards out of my pocket and started reading. I decided it didn't matter which dead guy I started with. One was as good as the next, really. I found my first candidate. Carlos Chavez of Chula Vista. He was a forty-five-year-old landscaper... stereotype... short, limited English, immigrant, a few petty crime arrests... an off-the-books temporary employee of his cousin's landscape company doing basic yardwork and clean-up gigs. Never made a mark on history. No school, no traceable long-term work record to speak of, no mentions in any newspaper article, no known associates... even his cousin didn't really know him. What is it gamers call those things, non-person character… NPC… invisible background figure for a video game? Going through life and never really accomplishing anything beyond being born and dying. But providing minimum wage manual labor, drinking beer, and watching Mexican soap operas on TV was fine for a lot of people. I'll never judge. Hell, he might have been happy. At least he wasn't a head-case drug-abusing drunk like me. He probably felt fulfilled and satisfied until some asshole took his life. Victim Chavez bought the farm in North Park… lot of weirdos in North Park. Stabbed in the neck… twice. A couple of the defensive knife wounds on his forearms and hands were diagrammed in the report. The neck wounds were perfectly fatal, like the perp knew where to strike.

I entered the address into my phone. The map popped up with a route. It was a short drive to where he was killed in an alley behind an old house that was used by an absentee owner as an internet hotel room... the app was called Air-Lodge. Amazingly, the detectives and officers assigned to the case didn't contact the owner for records on who was renting the place that day. Odd… I'd have to ask Rose about that.

Traffic was light. I cruised up through Hillcrest and cut over to North Park, passing out of the gay district and into Hipsterville.

I should pick up some of those chicken pot pies at that shop while I'm up here, I thought. Those are delicious.

I found the alley. There was still some faded plastic crime scene tape attached to a wooden gate by the trash cans. What was he doing back here? There was a green dumpster for lawn trimmings among the black generic trash and blue for plastic trash cans. Maybe it was shared by some neighbors. He must have been on a job.

Driving around to the front, I parked and watched the street for half an hour… not much activity, but you can get a feel for a neighborhood if you just sit and look at it for a while. They probably built the houses on this street around World War II. They were mostly two-story homes for big families. Each had a narrow single driveway that went to a separate garage in the back. Some were nicer than others, some were in disrepair, some were just invisible in their absence of uniqueness.

After thirty minutes I realized my coffee was gone, and the

ephedrine buzz was wearing off. I was getting a headache. I fished a bottled water out of my war bag and took some aspirin and a handful of allergy pills.

Feeling better.

I fished my tablet computer out of the bag and started doing searches on the Air-Lodge site until I found the house. I worked some bullshit magic on a couple levels of property management types and finally got in touch with the owner.

It was a guy from Cincinnati... People from Cincinnati are nice, trusting, and deserve respect. I usually go with that attitude when circumstances allow. But this was a case. So, I decided to lie my ass off and tell him I was a cop assigned the case at his little San Diego investment house.

"This is Detective Smith from the San Diego Police Department. I'm calling regarding your case here. Do you have a moment to discuss it?"

"I am surprised you haven't called before. I had to file an insurance claim for the damages."

He's chatty... nice.

"What damages, sir?"

"I tried to file a report of vandalism, but they just gave me a case number and said they would get back to me if necessary. Isn't that what this is about?"

"Yeah, sorry. Vandalism. Can you tell me what happened?"

"Guests apparently shot up the place. There were like six bullet holes in the walls and some broken furniture. And then they had drugs. The cleaning crew said it looked like they must have had a ton of marijuana in the place for the amount of seeds and stems on the floor. Not judging or complaining. I only needed a case number for the insurance claim. And I promise you, I really blasted them on the website. They'll never get another online vacation rental again."

The revelation surprised me. And I was even more surprised to learn that no one followed up on this in the homicide division.

"So, can you send me your file on the guests, please? I want to see if they damaged any other places." I tried to pique his interest, "This might be bigger than we thought." It was time to hook him with the old '*we're on the same team here*' routine. "We rarely discuss investigations, but I have an uncle in Ohio that I used to visit so..."

go Buckeyes… I feel like I can trust you… Between you and me, I'll let you know what's going on."

I could almost hear him beaming with pride.

"Where in Ohio?"

Well, shit.

I mumbled a vague word that sounded like an Ohio County thinking that a sort of native American sounding word might work.… "Kabungaho County… Up North… Northeast. Where the old factory thing is." I cleared my throat and excused myself as I said it, hoping that someone from Southern Ohio wouldn't know the Northeast part of the state any better than I did.

"Oh yeah," he lied unconvincingly. "Up North… the factory thing. The old uh… automotive plant."

He was guessing. I figured he didn't want to be stumped by a west coast cop on Ohio geography.

Agreeing with his bullshit was the right thing to do now in order to seal the deal. "Right."

Mr. Cincinnati went to super citizen mode and became extremely cooperative. "Sure. Anything for a fellow Buckeye… well, almost a Buckeye… Hey, I'm declaring you an official Buckeye. Where do I send it?"

"Why don't we have you mail it to me directly to my private email. That way none of this will get lost in the bureaucracy." I guessed that as a Midwesterner, he had an inherent distrust of government and bureaucracies. "Email it to me and I'll give you my direct phone line in case anything else comes up." I gave him a private email alias of *DetectiveSmithPD@gmail.com* and my anonymous online voicemail account phone number.

"I can see why they call you America's Greatest City. The customer service is great. I'm in advertising… shampoo and bathroom goods… Why, we are the biggest in the world, actually. A lot of people don't know we have offices here but…"

I cut him off. "Hey, I use shampoo… small world." I said, as authentically impressed as I could fake. "I'll hold while you send it."

I wasn't letting this knob off the line. Rookies sometimes rely on the witness to do police work for them without oversight and then later wonder why the citizen didn't follow through. I never let a witness out of my grimy little black leather gloved hands until I get everything I need.

"Great. I'm at my computer right now. Here it comes."

I waited a few seconds… Boom. The shit popped up on my screen. "Got it. Thank you for your cooperation and thank you for supporting American law enforcement. You are a, uh… substantial citizen."

I could almost see him grinning as his mind envisioned him telling all his friends he supported law enforcement, how he was a substantial citizen, and that he was working closely with the San Diego Police on a big investigation.

I fully realized that all the stuff he sent me would likely comprise mostly bogus bullshit, but in every pile of bogus bullshit, there is often a grain of useful fact. I'd print his shit up and take it to the beach later, when I had time to read and reflect. But there was one thing that seemed clear, the dead guy got whacked because of something he saw, not something he did. The separate garage in the back. Someone was using a weekend rental to move weight… I think I might have a dope case.

On to the next shit-show.

Body Number Three

I found the scene in about 20 minutes… This one was a warehouse near the shithole East Village. I parked by a brewery and locked up the car. There were bums loitering around, and I could feel them eyeballing me.

I needed to leave them a subliminal message. I wanted them to remember the lean, mean chick in the tight black denim jeans tucked in Rocky 911 SWAT boots with a Metallica T-shirt and a black leather jacket… I wanted them to remember how she slowly lit a cigarette and then pushed her jacket aside so she could stuff the lighter in her hip pocket. I wanted them to see the Glock 26 on my belt. Then I gave them the June Glume stink eye… each one of them.

A dirtbag who was clearly an alpha bum started to say something. I walked over and gave him a ten-dollar bill.

"Make sure none of these dickheads even breaths on my car and I'll trade you that ten for a twenty when I get back… thirty minutes at most."

He might be a bum, but he wasn't a dumb fuck like the rest of them sprawled out on the sidewalk, smoking ginger and sipping cheap wine.

"You got it, boss. Fuck these assholes."

"Clearly you are 'employee of the month' material… See you in thirty."

I walked over to the alley behind the warehouse, where the victim was bludgeoned to death. Bludgeon is a technical word we use in police work that means smashed to dog shit with a club or something.

There was still a little crime scene tape near the dumpster. This was definitely the spot.

I tried to imagine what could lead to a random beat down. The victim was a delivery man. He worked as a freelancer for various furniture companies and office supply stores. He was a nobody. Was it dope? Women? Theft?

Hard to say.

I glanced over the report notes.

The transporter victim's truck was missing.

Obviously, his truck was missing. Duh…

Victim's regular employers were not using him that day.

That means he wasn't jacked for a new office chair.

Victim was a Mormon.

That probably eliminates a few motives, like drugs or alcohol, unless he wasn't very good at being a Mormon. His record was totally clean… from the notes, it sounded like he was a good guy. He was probably a patsy who had no idea what he was getting into. Another innocent churned up in this shit-show.

Everybody has bills to pay. What if he took on a new client that no one else knew about? A client who offered a significant cash premium for doing the job. A new client who happened to be a nefarious dick. What if the victim saw something he wasn't supposed to see?

That made more sense than what the SDPD thought with their *'possible gang activity'* theory.

Shit.

I hate gangs. But I hate blaming everything that happens on gang activity. But it's easy to throw money at the gang industrial complex, the do-gooders, the specialty squads on the PD, the social programs, the army of consultants who know how to solve stuff but never do.

Maybe it's just me, but if gangs are so bad, just declare them terrorists and shoot them on site. Otherwise, just deal with the ones committing crimes. We often lose sight of the criminal offense in our love affair with complex conspiracies, enhanced sentencing, and headlines.

I'm losing it… going off track… I need a drink… I lost the balance. Too much central nervous stimulant without a counterbalance… But I needed my focus.

I took a few photos with my phone and walked back to the car. There was a bum there… oh yeah, that's my bum… *I need some stay-awake pills… and a drink… find the balance. Keep the focus…*

I pulled a twenty out of my pocket.

The bum saw me coming and spoke up. "Your car is fine, boss. All good."

"Let me ask you something. What's your name?"

"Roscoe… Roscoe Washington."

"Roscoe, I need to figure out why there was a dead guy behind the warehouse last month. Maybe three weeks ago. You know about it?"

"Yeah, I know about it. What's it worth to you to know about it too?"

"Twenty for car security and thirty for a little help. That makes it any even fifty."

"I don't do credit cards."

"Cash."

"Bankers."

"What? You want to go to the bank?"

What the hell is this guy talking about?

"No… bankers killed him… the ones that aren't a regular bank… I see their armored cars around town."

"Roscoe, that sounds like bullshit."

"Serious. The guy made a delivery. Saw too much. Then they smoked his ass. They killin' everybody… even *my* people are pissed off."

"The bums?"

"No." He appeared insulted. "Fuck the bums…. I'm talking about the hood. They're my people. These banker guys are driving drug prices up. Killing people… Weed getting too expensive."

"Fine… here you go." I handed my dubious source fifty bucks. I better ask Kimberly if I have an expense account. This could get pricey… especially bum information, which is seldom worth a shit.

I hopped back in my car in search of coffee, a drugstore, and a ride-share gig. In that order. But there was something to think about… *what could be transported that was worth killing a guy over? Dope or cash… I need coffee.*

CHAPTER 6

Ride share journal entry—June Glume

I sipped coffee and popped some over-the-counter stay-awakes. A ride appeared on the phone screen, a trip from Hillcrest to Shelter Island. I was close, so I took it. I'd been wanting to get out to Shelter Island for a while. The view was amazing, and the parks weren't overrun with bums. Maybe I'd kick back at the park after I dropped whatever knob I was hauling off to their destination.

I wheeled up to the front of the condo building. The rider was a young woman… maybe twenty years old. Cute… nicely dressed, casual but clean and crisp. She seemed like a human being… which was odd.

"Hi… I'm Sherry…. Going to the Harbor Resort on Shelter Island."

"I'm June. You got it."

Sherry got belted in and comfortable. Her eyes were clear, and she was coherent and engaging. I instantly went on alert… something was wrong here… shit… she didn't have her face buried in a cell phone. That is extremely unusual. Is she some kind of psychopath? At least we'd have something in common.

I could tell she wanted to talk. Generally, I hate talking. But she seemed nice. I let her start.

"How long have you been a ride-share driver?" Sherry asked the question I get asked a dozen times a day.

"Too long. I'm addicted to it."

She snickered.

"I can see how it would be super exciting, driving around beautiful San Diego, meeting new people every day, and hearing all their stories. You must make a lot of friends doing this."

"I'm not a people-person, Sherry. I'm a driver-person, I love to drive. That's what I'm addicted to, getting paid to drive."

"Oh… I'm totally a people person. I'm starting a new job at the resort as a reservation manager. I always wanted to be a reservation manager. This is so exciting."

"Where you from Sherry?" I asked. "The Midwest?"

"Winchester, Indiana."

"And you've only been in town about three weeks?"

"How did you know?" she giggled in amazement.

"The ride-share app tells us stuff, so we have something to talk to the passengers about," I lied.

"Oh, that is so smart… cool," she said, embracing my made-up invasion of privacy explanation.

We made our way down Rosecrans and out to Shelter Island. I dropped her at her new job.

"Bye, June. It was so nice to meet you," she chattered like a chipmunk on crack as she got out of the car. "I'm sooooo excited! Woo-Woo!"

Shit… a woo-woo girl.

"Good luck, Sherry." I said… and I meant it… but not the way she thought I meant it.

I drove further down Shelter Island towards that Japanese bell thing until spotted a piece of shade by the water. I parked, set up my folding chair I keep in the trunk, and kicked back. It was time to sip coffee and review my case cards, while taking in the scenery, of course.

A destroyer chugged into the bay. It made me miss my military service. At least there, the bosses didn't get so cranky when you kill people.

- End journal entry

Broadway and 10th

I thought about my findings as I drove. Driving allows me to think. I get rational behind the wheel. I suspect it's some cop thing. You stay sharp when you drive no matter how tired or even hungover you are. If you let your guard down, you might die.

But in the multiple-victim murder conspiracy case that was only a case because there was no evidence and no connections, I needed a connection.

The topic of weed came up more than once. Interesting… but why? Although, one of my sources who mentioned weed was probably nuts… but just because he's nuts, doesn't mean he's wrong. That's something young cops often learn the hard way.

Never dismiss a crazy bastard's information.

Yet why would someone kill over weed? It's basically legal now. I decided to pay a visit to my old pal Santos, the retired dope dealer currently residing in North Park. He used to snitch for me. I treated him fairly, and he stayed in touch. Snitches are human beings until they aren't. I treat them as such.

Forty minutes later, I banged on his door and he let me in.

"Glume? What the hell do you want?"

I ignored the .45 automatic he pointed at my face. Gun waving in Santos' inner-circle of scum was really more of a procedure than a threat.

"I come in peace, Santos. I got a question and I think you *might* be able to help me figure it out."

"I don't do the business anymore. Everything is legitimate. I have my garage and my dry cleaner and my eight laundromats. I'm totally legit."

I lit a cigarette to create a pause in the standoff. After taking a long drag, I made another attempt to convince him to cooperate. "Then how about a drink, moneybags?"

He laughed at my audacity and invited me in.

We did a tequila shot. It just so happened that he had a bottle and some shot glasses on his coffee table. They weren't clean glasses, but I don't care. Tequila will kill any germs, viruses, or diseases on the planet. It's an elixir of life in its own way.

After a couple of drinks, his curiosity about my presence got the best of him. "What's on your mind, June?" he asked.

"A puzzle. Why would someone kill over weed?"

"Unless it's weight, no reason."

"Let me reframe that, Santos. Why would someone kill a Columbian national over weed?"

He laughed and poured two more shots.

"Easy. It ain't the weed, it's the cash."

"What?"

He gave me a thirty-minute lecture on the topic.

Holy shit!

Death Metal Investigations – Coronado, California

Kimberly was on the phone when I walked in. She was placating someone about something.

"Rick, you should totally do it. People know your music, but they don't know you, but they should… I mean really, Hoochie Koo was a masterpiece… No, you're not too old… Look, I'll talk to a guy I know. I think he can put it together for you… Okay, got to run… Ciao."

She looked up and smiled. "Any luck, Glume?"

"More questions than answers, but I think there is a connection between these dead guys and some drug business."

"Cartel?"

"Maybe cartel financed, but I think it might be something legal."

"Legal?"

"Pot. It's the weed industry."

"Why would someone kill over weed?"

"Not the weed, the cash." I said, parroting Santos, the crime encyclopedia.

"What?"

"I'm taking some leaps here, but we got a dead rich business lady from Columbia, a dead guy who was working outside a possible stash house, and a dead guy who was possibly a transporter. Another guy who got himself whacked is a big shot realtor who was a known large cash donor and supporter of Proposition 215. None of that makes sense as a traditional cartel thing. I don't believe they're moving weight; they're moving cash."

"But cash is legal," she countered, obviously intrigued.

"Not moving more than ten thousand at a time… sans government paperwork."

"Oh yeah, I had to sign a bunch of forms when I got the first big payout. I didn't pay attention to what that shit was. So why weed? It could be anything."

"It's a hot ticket in San Diego now. They're making unimaginable amounts of cash."

"Wow… I had no idea."

"So much cash you have to weigh it instead of counting it. There was a guy in Colorado filling fifty-five-gallon drums with cash and he only had a couple of shops."

"No shit? So why not just put it in the bank and pay the taxes? They're loaded, it seems. They shouldn't feel much pain from the government bite."

"The banks are licensed federally, Kimberly. Weed is illegal federally, therefore no banks to pack the cash away into. They don't take weed money."

"I never heard that before… wow… it could be important."

"Yeah, the larger weed businesses buy old bank buildings and armored cars and do the cash runs themselves. Eventually it gets distributed and into the economy… or to Mexico. But it's still big."

"What makes you think this?"

"It just seems obvious, something hidden, something moved, something not cartel's style, and something worth killing over. Besides, I received some information from a reliable source."

"Whoa… sounds gnarly."

"I'll say… very gnarly… I think a drop was taken down, a shipment was taken down, and a main player was taken down to send a message."

"Dead lady on the Embarcadero?"

"Yeah, the dead lady on the Embarcadero… she was too smart to get killed."

"Apparently, the killer didn't review her IQ exam score before he blasted her with a shotgun. So, what does it all mean?"

"It means one thing. The pot boys got two problems. Columbian financing and a snitch on the inside of their operation who's going into business for himself. Could be a low-life or it could be a top-dog in the company embezzling. This is going to get ugly."

"Maybe we should drop it."

"Maybe we should double down."

Kimberly's face contorted into a twisted smile. "Yeah… what the hell. We're keeping it metal."

That response made June snort. Music industry people have no clue. This was going to get metal alright, and they'd need a guy.

"Kimberly, do we have money in the budget for another guy? I might need backup and I don't think you want to get killed."

"I got money to buy a police department. Who do you want?"

"There's a professional I know who goes by Raven. I'm going to need Raven on this."

Los Angeles, California – Law Office of Beauregard O. Gilpenny

"Just a minute, Mr. Gilpenny, I have to take this." Raven took the call.

"Raven, it's Glume. I need you for a job. It pays well and you'll probably get killed."

Raven didn't hesitate. "On my way. I'm with my attorney but I'll be done in five minutes." He popped the phone back in his pocket.

"Sorry, Mr. Gilpenny. It was someone I owe an enormous debt to."

"Financial or moral?" the attorney asked.

"Honor."

"I see. That seems to be a theme with you." Gilpenny smiled like an approving parent. "We're about finished here for today, so if you wish to take your leave to address your debt of honor, you may go knowing this matter is being addressed. I'll have Mr. Christianson locate the surviving gold-star family members and we shall collect for them what they are due from the Government. Mr. Christianson was a combat Marine, so he understands the importance of taking care of the family of a fallen brother-in-arms. Consider this done."

"The family deserved more respect. This wouldn't have happened with our favorite president," Raven observed.

Gilpenny agreed, "So true. We must support our military and first responders. It's a bit of a theme with me too," Gilpenny said in his famous deep baritone.

"Thank you, sir."

"Thank you, Raven. Godspeed."

Coronado, California - Death Metal Investigations

"So, who is this Raven," Kimberly asked?

"He's a bass player," I muttered, not happy about having to explain who the potential new guy was. It's not like I'd bring some feckless knob into the team.

A blink and a headshake. "What?"

I suspected she would question this recruitment. I haven't

learned how far I can go with her yet. But in my defense, you never really know how far you can go with anyone until you go too far. I attempted to make my new-hire more palatable, so I led with the angle of their common past. "You'll get along. He's a bass player. He had a metal band in the Houston area. Not a big following really, just regional, but he has a passion for it. You probably know a lot of the same people."

"I know a lot of musicians, but none of them are professional muscle. I thought you said we needed professional muscle?" Kimberly said accusingly, wondering if Glume was high.

I elaborated, "He's also a former Delta Force operator. Raven is six-foot-five, weighs two-seventy, and can bench press a buffalo. He served all over the world... and he owes me."

"He owes you what?"

"He was wrongly accused of killing a guy and I got him off. He blew into town a couple of years ago with no local ties, so he was an easy target for lazy detectives to hang a murder rap on. The thing is, he always wanted to be a musician rather than muscle for hire. So, you two have that in common."

I sensed my *'something in common'* theme was failing.

Kimberly frowned. "This gets better and better. So then, he's *not* a killer?"

"Oh no, he's totally a killer. He just didn't kill the guy they *accused* him of killing. He was looking at life in prison before I intervened... but he's a killer. After he left the military, where he was a rock-star sniper, he went private and took on freelance enforcer jobs between music gigs. The worst outlaw motorcycle gangs use him. The mob has used him. They really like him. Even prison gangs use him. But he only kills assholes. He wouldn't kill anyone nice. He's honorable like that."

"Sounds charming." Kimberly eye rolled.

"Charming isn't the word I'd use," I confessed.

"Luckily for your Mr. Raven, I have a thing for vets."

Another surprise. She didn't seem like she would dig the military scene.

I said, "He'll be here tomorrow. Briefing at ten?"

"How about ten-hundred-hours?" Kimberly suggested enthusiastically, eager to attempt some cop jargon.

"Uh... fine... ten-hundred."

"When is that again?" she asked.

"It's ten in the morning." I said blankly, enduring her awkward enthusiasm for the good of the company. A little patience on my part was appropriate. After all, she had enough faith in old June Glume to invest time and money in my investigative skills... skin in the game.

Kimberly seemed happy, "Cool... ten-hundred-hours then."

I needed some time behind the wheel to get my head straight. I'd pick up a few ride-shares and get in tune with the universe.

CHAPTER 7

Ride share journal entry—June Glume

I usually ignore the blathering of my riders, but I had a live one in the back seat, a progressive chatterbox. We hadn't gone two blocks before I knew he did cross-fit, was a feminist, was an environmentalist, and a supporter of some politician I never heard of. Oh, I almost forgot, he's also a vegetarian.

I don't follow politics, but I generally know how somebody votes if I drive them more than a mile. If they're friendly and mind their own business, they're usually leaning independent or conservative. If they are outraged, have the answer to everything, and can't wait to tell me, then I assume they're leaning a bit liberal. Sometimes the conservatives get a little rowdy and start bitching about Washington D.C. but having worked for the government in the Army and on the police department, I knew they were usually on the money. I just tune it out. But the guy in the back was starting to annoy me. I consumed only a few sips of coffee and zero drugs today, so I was not on my optimal plane of tolerance yet.

"I'm really surprised you don't use an electric car. You're poisoning the atmosphere with this thing," he loudly explained, making a face of disapproval as he looked around the interior of my car.

He switched gears.

"Electric is the car of the future. And they are more affordable than ever. You can recharge them at a lot more places now. You need an electric car.

I took a quick glance in the rear-view mirror. He was smiling like he was an attorney who just won a seven-figure settlement for a slip-fall in a drugstore.

I don't care about other people's politics. I only care about my own. But I don't really like someone who accepts a ride with me in my car, and then insults me and my car. Dick move.

He kept it up. "As a woman, I would think you would care

more."

A police car running code three rolled past us as I took the curb to let it by.

"Pig!" He snorted. "Cops are murderers. All cops are bastards," he grumbled.

I thought it was weird that a middle-aged man in nice business attire would be so vocal, but then he told me he was from San Francisco, which would explain his having the social maturity of a horny tweener.

"We're a little more into enlightenment there," he elaborated. "We're in touch with nature and understand policy."

I was just trying to get this gasbag to his destination and do my job, but I really felt like dumping him off in the middle of gang territory and letting him explain his enlightenment to some of the homies.

He switched gears again. I guess he wanted to hit all of the commie bullet points before he got to his destination.

"Obviously, you agree that protecting the ocean is the most important issue of our time. You're a woman, so you'd be more in touch with nature than others. I try to stay in touch with my feminine side. Did I mention I'm a feminist?"

"You didn't have to mention it sir, it shows." I said deadpanned.

"Thank you!" He giggled as he basked in the glory of his virtue superiority.

I declined to mention I was in the Army and in the cops. In those circles, we could give a shit less what someone is. It was all about doing the job. Not to say there wasn't chatter among us that would make this worm poop in his suit pants. Our dark humor crosses lines that appall people like my candy-assed passenger. But it's what kept us sane.

"Here's your hotel, sir. Enjoy your stay in sunny San Diego."

"Oh, I'm not here to enjoy it. I'm representing an animal-rights group that is suing one of your local amusement parks. I can't wait to get back to San Francisco. We're a little more enlightened up there."

Like I forgot how enlightened they are...

He hopped out of my car and walked up to the bellman of his five-star resort hotel.

I put a block on him for any future rides with me.

I can't say that I'll miss this jack-ass.
  - *End journal entry*

Coronado, California - Bird's Nest Café – Orange Avenue

I relaxed at a sidewalk table with two cups of coffee, waiting for Raven. It had been a while since we last met face to face. Therefore, I felt like I should catch up with him first before taking him to the office to meet our boss. People change. Sometimes extreme people change extremely. It would be good to get a read of where his head is now. He texted me he would be five minutes late, so I was sneaking sips out of my cup. The coffee I purchased for us wasn't fancy, it was what the owners of the cafe call a 'batch brew' which in English means black drip coffee.

Soon a monstrous looking black four-wheel-drive truck rolled up and parked at the curb. It was a thing of beauty, the new Dodge Rebel with the Night Edition trim, definitely a beast.

Raven stepped out. He was a beast too, just like I remembered him. Mean looking and tough. He really didn't fit into the Coronado beach scene. The hulking veteran was wearing a black t-shirt, black jeans, black cowboy boots, maybe ostrich leather, and pirate scarf looking thing on his head. He was decked out like a Christmas tree with decorations, if by decorations one means stainless steel skulls on bracelets and rings. His long black hair always made me wonder if he was part Native-American. But I think he was pure red neck.

"Glume," he grunted. "How are you?"

I gave him a sisterly hug. "I'm still alive."

He gave a disinterested hug back. Raven was not an affectionate person.

"So, those assholes kicked you out of the cops over my shit, didn't they," he stated flatly.

"Yeah, you like to get right to the point, don't ya, dude."

I must have appeared defensive in my response to his opening comment. He visibly lightened up.

He rephrased his question into a sentiment. "That's a shame. I sincerely mean that. You were good at it."

"Thanks, Raven."

Raven shifted gears to business. "What do you need from me?"

Again, right to the point.

So, I got to the point. "I'd like you to work for Death Metal Investigations. I'm a private nose now. We got funding so there ain't no lean months in our future."

"Death Metal Investigations?"

He seemed confused. I could understand why.

"Yeah, it's a licensed firm run by a lady named Kimberly Tyler. You might know her."

"I know of a Kimberly Tyler. But she was a roadie… not a detective."

"That's her. She came into some money, and we started the company."

"Wow… she crewed for Metallica, Iron Maiden, and even Jimmy Buffett… if I remember correctly, she could do about anything, but mainly ran transport and logistical stuff. Smart lady. I thought she died or something. Haven't heard of her for years."

"Yeah, I don't know much about that part of her history. I think she lived a couple more lives between then and now. You two can figure that out if you want. But now she's my benefactor and the owner of the company so, I'm all in."

He looked at me quizzically. "So, you been doing this since, uh… *'you know'* happened…" avoiding the obviously touchy subject of my abrupt departure from law enforcement.

"No, this is new. I've been doing ride-share, some security gigs when they come up. Just getting by."

"Well, you are one of the most honest people I know, and I owe you a lot. Not just a debt, but I owe you my freedom. I never forget people who done right by me."

"Raven, if I recall correctly, you never forget people who done wrong by you either."

"Guilty." He gave me a hint of a sheepish smile. It was almost endearing coming from such a big nasty-looking son-of-a-bitch.

"It might involve some rough stuff. Cartel, Columbians, drugs…" I cautioned.

"Meh."

"Let's go meet Kimberly."

We took our coffees, walked across the street and around the corner to the office.

Death Metal Investigations – Downtown Coronado, California

Kimberly stood. "Welcome to the clubhouse, Raven." She extended a hand.

Raven shook her hand firmly and once again got to the point. "Thanks, so what's the deal?"

Kimberly might be chatty in social situations, but she preferred getting down to it when it came to business. She seemed adept at being chatty at the right time and blunt at the right time.

"Glume needs a partner on the street. A seventy-five grand a year plus expenses. You'll take orders from her."

"That's too much money."

Kimberly grinned. "You're a tough negotiator, Raven. What sounds fair to you?"

"How about you lease me a furnished studio apartment in Little Italy and very plain car under a fake company name and give me twenty-five hundred a month to live on plus expenses? If I make you money, give me a cash bonus. I'd prefer to remain off the grid."

"Okay."

"And if I get a gig with a tour, I'll need to quit or go on leave. I have nothing in the works right now, but you never know."

"What about local gigs?"

"I don't have one."

"If I can get you one, will you stay local?"

"Sure, I just want to do a show once in a while."

"Done. I'll have one of my lawyers take care of the apartment and car." She reached into a desk drawer and pulled out a wad of cash. She gave me some of it and gave Raven what appeared to be an equal sum. "Here's ten-thousand each, it's a recruitment and recruiting bonus. I'll have all the other stuff done by the end of the week. Good enough?"

Raven grunted what might have been agreement.

I piped in on Raven's behalf. "More than fair, boss."

"Then you two get to work. I'm having lunch with one of the Farriss brothers. He's in town, so we are having a little reunion. Oh, and June, this is for you. Raven, I'll hook you up later." She pushed a little carton of business cards towards me.

I took the cards, but I had no idea who she was talking about.

But I noticed Raven perked up a bit. He said nothing, but I sensed she impressed him with her social circle.

"Thanks." I said. I looked at Raven as I stuffed the cards in my pocket. "Raven, do you want to go celebrate over a beer at Danny's? We can brief tomorrow on the case."

"Sounds good," he grumbled out.

As we got up, Raven asked Kimberly an unexpected question. "What's your cat's name?" he asked, pointing to the black feline stretched out on her desk.

"Sabbath."

If it was anyone else but Raven, I would say his face creased in the form of a smile. "Black Sabbath. I like it. Not normally a cat lover, but this one rocks."

I snickered, never having thought to ask about the cat before. I don't give a shit about cats, but now that Raven brought it up, it was kind of cool. Company mascot, I suppose. But there was something mysterious about it. I guess that is a common characteristic of black cats. They carry a metaphysical vibe that is simultaneously friend and foe.

We all left the office together. Raven and I drank an early lunch. Kimberly went to her meeting.

Tomorrow would be a busy day.

DEA Task Force headquarters – San Diego County

"So, chief, it appears that a crew of enforcers are either on their way here from El Salvador or they might have actually been here already for a couple of months. Our sources are tight. What we don't know is why." The Special Agent in Charge gazed across the conference room table with world-weary eyes at the near-shoulderless excuse of a police chief.

"Special Agent Luna, I don't know what you expect for us to do. We can do some community outreach, perhaps a Tic-Toc or Instagram video to warn the public but if they haven't committed a crime, the police have no authority."

The Agent said nothing as he tried to control his breathing and reduce his blood pressure. The noodle-armed police chief of America's 6th largest city was better suited to run a drum circle, but he'd probably fuck that up to. Luna couldn't understand the chief's aversion to conflict with criminals while he steadily pushed social issues that conflicted with the vast majority of San Diegans.

"Chief, you can do what you want. All I really want to accomplish in this meeting is sharing our intelligence with you. We have a crew of assassins from Columbia who have either been here for a couple of months or are on their way here. If you know why this might be happening, we'd love to help you with it."

"This sounds Federal. I'm not sure we should be involved."

"You pulled your detectives out of our joint task force a year ago. Will you consider sending an officer back? We're trying to work with you here."

"I don't like enforcing laws. That's not what we're here for."

Luna tried another approach. "Well, can we perhaps liaison with someone from homicide to track potentially related crime?"

"I can't see how that would help. Our homicide people are focusing on police violence now and can barely keep up their caseloads on regular murders and robberies. You're on your own. Sounds like a Federal problem."

"It's a San Diego problem, Chief."

"What's that supposed to mean?"

"It means what it means..." Luna took a deep breath before he burned the feeble bridge between his agency and the Chief any more than it was already, "Look, we will handle our side of it. I'll just ask you to keep the details of this meeting confidential."

"Other than my briefing to the City Council Crime Committee, I'll not discuss it with anyone else."

The DEA agent stared blankly. *Might as well have briefed the cartel directly then.*

Luna wasn't one to waste time. He abruptly stood up, shook hand with the chief, thanked him for his cooperation, while stepping towards the door.

What soft hands he has for a man, Luna thought as he strode back to his office to try to come up with a Plan B.

The Midnight Hour Diner, Orange Avenue, Coronado California

The next morning, I talked while Raven worked over a pancake the size of a hubcap. "My conclusion is that foreign actors invested big money in the local marijuana industry, and someone is siphoning it into their own pocket and trying to hide it with a series of random crimes."

"So, who?"

"Perhaps competing local investors using outside, possible foreign muscle to secure some margin in the industry, or perhaps just local managers embezzling."

"So various cartels are going to war over weed?" He sounded skeptical.

"No. Not weed. The cash from weed. Think about it, Raven. Millions, if not billions, at stake. Staged rip-offs to cover up embezzlement. Possibly an auditor whacked, possibly witnesses whacked. We just need to figure out which dispensary company is behind it and then sort it out."

"How do we do that?"

"We work informers, we ask the cops who are still *real* cops, and maybe we put the bag on a dispensary business insider and squeeze them."

"I choose all the above," Raven said through a mouthful of pancake.

"That works for me. I'll get some names and we can go to work."

Raven polished off half of a cup of coffee in one huge gulp and signaled for a refill. "Let me get one more cup and I'll get your information for you. Just point me in the right direction."

"I love that can-do attitude, Raven."

"I'm an American. Can-do is what we do." He gave a brief salute to the portrait of Marcus Latrell that was hanging on the wall. Coronado was a SEAL town and almost every business, with the exception of the gluten-free muffin store and one of the yoga studios, had some kind of Navy memorabilia on the walls.

"Let's roll."

San Diego PD - Homicide

Rose shuffled through paperwork while trying to remember what it was like to have a fully staffed squad room. The chronic staff shortages were taking their toll. All there was time for was reading and signing with little time available for investigating and arresting. She paused and stared at the folder on the dead woman at the Embarcadero as she sipped some coffee.

She pushed her other paperwork aside and opened the file. It was time to forget what happened and focus on who it happened to. There had to be something on the woman that could be of help. She wrote a page of notes in longhand on a yellow legal pad as she reviewed the file. She snapped a photo of her notes and emailed it to June. Maybe *she* had a connection who could help.

Frowning, she put the case file away again and resumed the tedium of digging through cases she would never have time to solve.

Her phone rang.

Death Metal Investigations – Coronado, California

I waited three rings before I heard her voice.

"Homicide, Detective Lopez."

I was in a hurry so I cut the pleasantries. "Rose, It's June."

"June? Is this about the photo?"

"What photo?" I asked. I attempted to try to see if I had a photo while talking on a voice call, but it was too much trouble and I didn't want to risk dropping this conversation.

"I just sent you a photo."

"No, I'll check it later…" Before I could continue, Rose cut me off with her signature whining-voice.

"What do you want? Last time we talked, you never called me back." She said in a strange blend of an accusation and whining. She was right, though.

"I need information." I answered, ignoring her complaint. No time today to listen to Rose whine.

"On what?" Rose responded resignedly.

I pressed. "Can you tell me the names of the top three players in the legal marijuana dispensary business community?"

"No."

"Why?"

"Because I don't know who that is."

Why would she? No one at the PD talks to each other anymore… too risky.

"Shit... Do you know who would?"

After a brief pause, she came up with a name. "Luna, DEA would know."

"I remember Luna… total stud." In police circles, stud can mean 'bad ass' or it can mean a 'male hottie.' The former is used by mostly the guys, but latter is used almost exclusively by the female coppers. I talked to him a few times. We had even discussed getting a drink, but it never happened. I like Luna. I doubt if he remembered me. Which was sad.

Rose knew what exactly I meant by the term stud. "Yeah, that's him. The Latin Fabio."

"The Latin who?"

"Never mind, but he would know if anyone would." She made a snort sound for some reason. *Disgust or approval? Who knows with Rose?*

"What about our guys in narcs?" I asked and immediately regretted phrasing words that made me sound like I was part of the PD again. They aren't *our* guys. I'm out. No longer a part of the family.

Rose didn't pick up on it. "Our dope squad guys aren't allowed to contact or interact with the dispensaries because of community relations bullshit."

What the hell?

"Really? What makes them any different from the other businesses that operate in the city?"

Rose explained, "The dispensaries are one of the many protected species of the woke-world, June. It's the way of the age of Aquarius I guess."

"I thought the age of Aquarius was the sixties."

"Whatever."

"Is there anybody else who *doesn't* carry a badge who might know something?" I asked, considering outside resources.

"Well, there's that crackpot Gillespie." Rose offered.

"The conspiracy theory guy who always writes letters to the editor?"

I met him a few times. Not a bad guy, really.

Rose elaborated. "He's kind of a nut, but more than half the time, he's right. In fact, he's almost always right… it's kind of creepy. He wrote quite a few letters claiming he had evidence that the cartels were behind the dispensaries and not local business owners."

"Yeah, but he also wrote a letter to the editor last week claiming a bunch of neo-druids camping near the Palomar Observatory are planning on signaling Mars so they can surrender earth so we can avoid a war with Mars."

"Actually, that is true. There are a bunch of weirdos from Baltimore who call themselves neo-druids and are trying to contact Mars. But *he* doesn't believe they will start a war. He just wants to avoid another mass-suicide sneaker people thing like we had a few years back. Remember that one? "

I had to shake my head at that one. "Holy crap, what is wrong with people?"

All we need is a war with some assholes from space… as if California isn't screwed up enough already.

"Did you miss the part about them being from Baltimore?" Rose explained.

It was my turn to snort. "You got a point. I'll talk to Gillespie and see what he's got."

Baltimore sucks. I heard some guys yelling in the background on her end.

Rose had to cut it short. "Look, the Sergeant and I have to go brief the Crime Committee at City Council about my case progress… Good luck, Junie… Let's get coffee again soon."

"Sounds good. I'll look at your photo and get back to you."

Commerce Bank Building - 5th Avenue, San Diego, California

"I always wanted to look around this place," Raven whispered as he looked around the one-hundred-and-thirty-year-old building.

"It's a landmark. They say Wyatt Earp used to own it and ran a whorehouse and gambling hall out of here called the Golden Poppy."

"Sweet." Raven quickly switched gears from sight-seer back to investigator, "So, this guy we are seeing has legit information? I thought you said he's a crackpot."

I answered Raven's question as we awaited the elevator to take us to the third floor. "He's a conspiracy theorist who has an independent publishing business here. He puts out books about all kinds of weird shit."

"And he has legit information?"

"That's what's creepy. On anything that *can* be proven, he always turns out to be right."

"Great. Just what we need, a psychic. Have you met this guy?"

"When I was in patrol division, I took a couple of reports from him, so I have talked to him a few times. He seems alright. He's super smart, but he's different. I doubt if he would remember me, though. That had to be ten years ago."

I banged on the door with the words 'Shadow World Publishing' centered on the near opaque frosted glazing.

"Come in," a deep masculine voice bellowed from behind the door. Those two simple words rang with the tenor of a polished public speaker. It was a voice that commanded respect.

I gently swung the door open and stepped in. Before I could open my mouth, the man sitting behind the desk stated, "June Glume. Welcome to Shadow World Publishing. What's it been, ten years?" He hopped out of his chair and came around to shake hands.

Apparently what Raven saw startled him enough to blurt out loud what he was thinking, "He's a fucking midget."

Gillespie snapped a reply, "We prefer to be called little people, dickhead."

Raven automatically reacted in his default belligerent mode, "Fine with me, little people dickhead."

I looked over my shoulder and shot Raven the *'don't even'* look, a talent I inherited from my mother. "Show some respect, Raven. We're in his house." I was surprised things didn't get ugly faster. Two leather clad bad-ass goons who look metal as fuck and a little person in a vintage gray business suit and fedora seemed like the perfect situation for a misunderstanding of the minds.

Raven took a deep breath as he processed his faux pas. "Sorry, Mr. Gillespie. I just don't see that many of you folks. That was a total dick move on my part. I might be an asshole, but I try not to be a dick. Respect and apologies, sir."

Gillespie sustained his rage face for another two seconds before he also took a deep breath. "Forget it. I'm sixty years old. I've heard it all and at this point in my life, could give a shit less. Sit down."

I spoke up as we sat in the elegant wood and leather straight-back office chairs. "I'm surprised you remembered me. It has been about ten years."

"I forget nothing, Miss Glume," he superciliously stated.

"Neither do I," I admitted, acknowledging my own curse of near total recall.

"Who is your friend?" he asked, as if my colleague wasn't there.

Raven spoke for himself. "They call me Raven."

"Raven what?"

"I just go by Raven... Like I explained before, I'm an asshole and I work for June and her partner at Death Metal Investigations."

"I appreciate your blunt and cogent introduction, sir. Now, how might I help you today?" He asked as he returned to his chair.

Leaning forward in the amazingly comfortable antique side chair, I handed Gillespie a business card as I stated our intent, "We're trying to learn about the marijuana dispensary business in San Diego. Who are the big players?" I tugged my well-worn LAPD-style leather notebook out of the inside pocket of my jacket. It made Gillespie smile. From the look of his office, he enjoyed and appreciated old-school stuff and old school style. Nothing is more old-school than the top-flip leather notebook used by detectives of lore. Mine appeared well worn, yet well cared for... I like nice stuff and I always do the work required to keep my things in top condition.

He hopped off his chair again and started pulling file folders out of an ancient wooden cabinet in the corner.

I looked around the room, admiring his photograph collection. Faded framed black and white images of him with famous faces adorned one wall. I recognized Buzz Aldrin, Stephen Hawking, Donald Trump, Calvin Klein, and Art Bell. What an eclectic group. On the other wall was a grand oil painting of Edgar Allan Poe with a black cat in his lap that must have been five-feet wide and six-feet tall.

"That is an amazing piece of art," I said as I took in the larger-than-life size portrait of the man with the black cat.

What's with the black cats in my life all of the sudden? I don't own a cat. I'm not even interested in cats. Now they're everywhere. Should I be creeped out?

"Thank you. I painted that one about thirty-years ago. It's one of my favorites."

Color me impressed. A conspiracy theorist who knew celebrities and had incredible artistic talent. The eyes were so cold, yet realistic. I felt like Poe was staring directly at me, or perhaps through me. Gillespie captured the mystery and horror generated by Poe's work perfectly.

His desk had a notebook computer and a larger computer workstation on the right side. He had a leather-bound binder and a beautiful fountain pen on the left side.

"I might have something for you, Miss Glume," he said as he hopped back up in his chair. "Please have a look at this."

"What is it?" I asked.

"A group I am loosely affiliated with has been monitoring the cash flow in these dispensary businesses. There are of course a few independent operators who bootstrapped their business, but most are connected to three big donors to the legalization proposition from two years ago." Gillespie explained. "The silent partners in one group included a local real estate tycoon, an investment banker, and a middle-aged trust fund baby. It appears they were the front for outside money that might have come from overseas sources. But this puzzle is only a very shallow view."

I leaned over the desk and saw a series of graphs and charts that were a little difficult to understand, especially reading upside down.

Gillespie smiled and reached under his desk. A glass panel slide out from the side of the desk and one of the TV screens on the wall lit up. Gillespie placed the first document on the glass, and it immediately appeared on the screen.

Raven whispered, "Cool."

Gillespie allowed a brief smirk to dance on his lips. He continued talking, using the fountain pen as a pointer which we could see on the screen. Raven was right. He was cool.

"Deleting the true 'traditional small business' operations from the equation, here are the principal investors, here are the businesses they operate, and here are the businesses listed in order of reported revenue."

I felt like I was back in community college, except this was interesting and useful. Gillespie laid out the industry like an Army

General lecturing on Gettysburg.

"So, although there appears to be multiple groups, there are in reality, only two. One group is funding ninety percent of the dispensary trade and the other is funding five percent. The five percent group is made up of either bootstrap or angel funded local small businesses. It might seem like there are more locals to the disinterested eye, but in reality, many of these so-called local small businesses are merely paper front businesses which are fully funded and owned by the big investment group. The controlling organization used mostly foreign money, probably Columbian and Chinese investments, and the group relies on a local political figure who keeps off the radar, another silent partner. It's an all-cash operation, a money launderers dream. The political figure hasn't been identified and no one, other than the group I'm loosely affiliated with, seems interested in him, not the FBI or the California Justice Department... nobody."

"Wow... I had no clue about this. Amazing..." I said as I scribbled notes.

"One more fun mystery... there is a rumor on the street that there was a document outlining the financials. It proved that the local kingpins were skimming vast amounts from their foreign investors... which could be bad news. They'd want that document back at all costs."

Raven had a good question. "What's this political figure provide in exchange for control of that foreign money?"

"Undermining of law enforcement, an inside ear to any potential political blow-back, and probably years of experience in bribes, treachery, and treason."

"So, who is our mysterious politician?" Raven asked, posing another good question.

"Unfortunately, the field for backstabbing, evil, opportunists, in California politics is too broad to pinpoint at this time," Gillespie stated flatly. "I refuse to make an accusation without solid evidence."

"How about this real estate guy, then?" I asked. "What's his story."

"Dead."

"My real estate homicide victim was a competing investor?"

"That would be the obvious answer, but I believe the late

gentleman was a partner of our political player," Gillespie said with an exhale of a man who might know too much.

I played nice and shared. "The cops have nothing on this. It's well on its way to eventually landing in the cold case files."

Raven spoke up again, "Who was real estate guy's number two?"

I liked that question. Raven thinks like a cop.

"The trust fund baby. He lives in Orange County. A gentleman by the name of Jason McHale. He's quite a piece of work, which I'm sure you will soon discover." Gillespie bestowed us with a conspiratorial smile.

I loved this guy.

I had to ask. "Have you ever thought about being a private investigator, Mr. Gillespie?"

That made him chuckle. It was good to break the mood of the grim presentation.

"To be honest, I have been considering getting in on the solution side of the equation rather than living out my remaining years on the problem-identification side. If you have an opening, keep me in mind," he said with a broad grin. "I no longer require a salary. I've done well with my investments and my publishing business. I think it would be good for me to join a team at my age, rather than continue playing the Lone Ranger… perhaps like a Lone Raven?" he added with a subtle smile.

Raven sat up in his chair and offered a knuckle bump to Mr. Gillespie. He accepted and returned the gesture.

Peace in our time.

I answered, interrupting their reconciliation moment. "I'll mention your availability to our boss. Anything else we should know, Mr. Gillespie?" I queried.

"One thing."

His grin deflated into a frown faster than a tire running over a stop-strip.

"What's that?" Raven asked.

His next words were chillier than an executioner's kiss goodbye.

"The Columbians are coming."

CHAPTER 8

Cassidy's Pub – Gaslamp Quarter, San Diego

Raven and I sipped beer as we went through the case from top to bottom. The information I'd picked up on this shit-show had been pretty accurate so far. We finally had the big picture. A good old Southern California turf war, complete with double-cross, was underway with the underbelly bottom-feeders of the crime world, the Columbian cartel, coming up to level the playing field with their reliable scorched earth policy.

Raven guzzled half a pint of a black beer, wiped his mouth with his sleeve, and placed the glass back on the table. "At least we have a real human to squeeze, Glume."

I agreed. "Yeah, I'll let Kimberly know we are going to Orange County. The packet Gillespie gave us on Trust Fund McHale is better than anything I ever received from the intelligence unit."

"Intelligence Unit? On the PD?" Raven asked.

"Army and PD both... but we *did* have one brilliant analyst on the PD. Old Dave. He had skills. I think he retired and moved to Texas or something... probably still snooping through open-source files and cataloging intel though." *I try not to think about the PD, but there were some good people there. I hate to admit that I miss them.*

Raven nodded. "That sounds about right. Good analysts never really retire; they just find other retired analysts and spend the rest of their lives trying to figure out the all the shit their bosses have been preventing them from uncovering while they were on the job. The good ones love stirring the shit."

"You got that right."

"So, what all do we have on our Orange County trust-fund maggot?"

"In a word, he's an asshole. To my knowledge no one has been able to identify a soul on earth who likes this worthless turd. He hangs out at the Bay Club on the Mariner Mile, has a forty-six-foot yacht he spends most of his time aboard, and lives in a big house on top of Spyglass Hill overlooking the ocean and the golf course. Did I mention he drives a Bentley?"

Raven interrupted. "Of course, he does."

I continued, "He is a possibly gay, not that it makes any difference other than he might be subject to blackmail. No known female partners. He's involved in funding local radical leftist groups."

"Damn commies," Raven muttered.

"No shit," I affirmed. I started working potential theories. "So if he's gay, could there have been something going on between him and Mister dead real-estate guy?"

"Unclear."

"We need to eliminate the possibility of a lovers' quarrel."

"True." I replied as I kept reading.

"Is that it on him?" Raven asked.

"He also has one arrest and conviction for abusing an animal."

Raven frowned at hearing the last bullet point, "When we're done with the case, I'm going to go ahead and kill him then," he said as calmly as if he said he was going to go outside and check the mailbox.

"No argument from me, brother, unless I happen to take his animal-abusing ass out first."

I flipped a page in the file and continued.

"Raven, we need to dig deeper into his phone records. He's not careful. According to what we have now, he's called Bogota Columbia four times and the DEA at least three times in the past year."

We both knew what that meant.

"He's definitely an asshole," Raven observed.

"Yep, working both sides of the street. We-might need his DEA contact at some point. That person could be tough to identify."

Raven agreed, "I'll put out some feelers. I have connections with some vets who joined DEA after they left the service. They might be able to find out something off the record."

I sensed potential trouble. "Tell them to be discreet. The agent on these calls is possibly compromised."

"Copy that."

"What do you say we take a cruise up to Orange County tomorrow and visit McHale on his yacht?"

"Outside the public eye is always good for conversations. Let's get up there early. I suspect he isn't a morning person. We'll catch him off guard."

"I can pick you up. How about we meet at Old Town at six in the morning… this will be fun."

"Cool."

I settled the tab as I watched Raven walk out of the pub. I asked for a receipt. This was definitely a business expense. As I signed the bottom of the merchant copy of the credit card receipt, I glanced at my watch. I had time to get a couple of rides in before I went home. Doing some ride-share would get me mentally prepared for tomorrow.

Ride share journal entry – June Glume

I saw a pickup at the Hilton Gaslamp. It was only a few blocks away.

The three passengers were waiting at the curb.

Shit.

Zoomers, the infamous 1997-2012 birth year knobs who are presently destroying the world as we know it.

I rolled down the passenger window as I pulled up to the curb. One of them leaned in to talk. "We're going to Petco Park."

That made no sense. "Are you sure you want a ride? It's two blocks. It's that building right there." I pointed at the looming ballpark at the end of K street. I felt obligated to tell them in case they were confused as to where it was. What kind of idiot takes a two-block ride-share on a beautiful early evening in San Diego?

On the sidewalk, another guy from the group stood vaping and intently gazing into his smart phone. He just looked like a typical pussy. I don't think he heard me. I'm not sure he even knew his ride had arrived. He was zoned out, deep in the alternate-reality dimension of the smart-phone.

An overweight girl with purple hair, short shorts, and a tube-top didn't approve of my suggestion. "Lady, it's your job to like… drive and stuff. You need to mind your own business."

Her female companion, who I think was trying to dress like a dude but ended up looking like an effeminate Peewee Herman, piped in with her hands on her hips and scolded me, "We don't need advice from the hired help. Just drive boomer. I'm in customer service. I'm a professional. I know not to be rude to customers. It's insulting."

I'm not a boomer. I'm a Gen Y... I like Boomers, they taught me everything I know and put Americans on the moon... But I'm not a Boomer. This little twenty-one year of twit just called me an old lady and then tried to riot act me. Not happening!

I stepped out of the car.

My face gave away my inner-rage. I guess it's outer-rage now. I got in Peewee's face.

"You're not in my car yet, asshole. So here is a piece of free advice. Take Chunky Madonna and Justin Beaver there and walk your sorry asses down the street. You're in my town. I got friends here who will stab your ass for a quarter. So beat it... and remember to pick up a twelve pack of humility and chug it right away because you ain't paid enough dues yet to talk to me that way, you disgusting little worm." I wondered which vein would explode first, the one in my forehead or the one in my neck.

Justin Beaver beamed back down to reality and joined the conversation now. "Who's Madonna?"

I popped a cigarette in my mouth and lit it with my old zippo while the wise-ass Zoomer shook in her shoes. I blew some smoke in his face. "Beat it shit heel."

The four of them scampered down the street like good little children.

I sat on the trunk deck of the car and finished my smoke.

I'm pretty sure they weren't veterans.

If they report me, I'll just tell the company that they were puking and drunk, so I refused them transport. I seldom lie to my bosses. But I would in this case.

- *End journal entry*

On the way home my cell phone rang... unpublished number... if it was a spam, the screen would indicate so. I took the call.

"This is Glume."

"June, this is Tom Patterson... homicide."

What the hell? "How can I help you, Tom?" I asked guardedly.

"Can you come to C Street and 5th... Something happened. I know you were friends..."

"Wait... what? What happened? I felt my heart beating hard in my chest like a base drum in a marching band.

"Rose was the victim of a street robbery. She's deceased."

I hit the mute button and jerked the wheel to a hard right to the curb.

Patterson's words were spoken kindly and professionally, but they burned through my soul. As a woman who worked in a man's world, I have a veneer, a tough veneer, but underneath I'm still a human being. Men are too, but they are wired to bury it deeper. It's why they die sooner than us. The load collapses their soul... Rose was my friend. I loved her. She was kind and everything I wanted to be, but couldn't. And now she's dead... how can this be? I'm the asshole. I should be dead. I have no family... I should be the one who is dead... Tears flowed. I had to pull over.

"Are you there?" Patterson asked.

"I'll be there in ten minutes."

C Street and 5th

I parked in the old NBC building garage and walked the two blocks over. I needed to clear my head before I talked to the detectives. At the yellow tape barricade, an officer working the perimeter met me with a clipboard. He was an old guy, a good street cop. I knew and respected him. Harold 'Slam' Jackson wasn't afraid to bust a head on the street or comfort a tearful elderly victim in his arms. His blood ran PD blue. He closely resembled that Hightower dude on the police academy movies, but bigger. If I recalled correctly, he did a stint as a professional wrestler after he got out of the Navy and before he joined the police department.

Jackson offered a sincere condolence. "Glume. I'm sorry. I knew you too were close."

His condolences surprised me. I didn't know anyone knew we were friends. But Rose probably blabbed to everyone about everything. She considered the police department to be her second family... and she felt she was responsible for the family newsletter.

"Thanks, Jackson. She was a good person. Patterson asked me to come by."

"Sign the log. He's over there." Jackson, a big man, pointed with his meaty finger towards a blue tarp on the sidewalk around the corner surrounded by a scrum of cheap suits.

I spotted Bridges over talking to some reporters. He saw me too. He covertly flipped me off. I returned the gesture.

Fog set in, typical here this time of year. I could make out Rose's left hand outside the edge of the tarp… like it was reaching for me. Like she was calling for help. It was hard, but I held my feelings in check. I'd been doing that for years at crime scenes. This was the most difficult one I ever experienced though. Rose needed me and I wasn't there.

What were my last words to her? Was I a bitch? Did I take out my failings on her? She deserved a better friend. Nobody ever knows that until it's too late.

Patterson interrupted my shame spiral. He spotted me and waved me over.

"Glume."

"Patterson."

We both stared at the tarp a moment before he continued speaking. "So sorry about your friend. She was a good cop."

I asked what I had to ask. "What happened?"

"It might be random. She was walking over to the Gaslamp to grab some dinner after a city hall briefing. It looks like a routine knifing and robbery. The perp came up from behind. She didn't have a chance."

"What's missing?"

"Her gun, purse, and her case file."

"Which case?"

"That fiasco with all the dead bodies downtown. She thought it was connected. I doubt it. But she was convinced. Nobody else was."

The bastard snorted and shook his head when he said nobody believed her. Not in a way as though it was sad that she had no support for her theory, but as if she was a fool. I'd remember that.

Bridges didn't appear to appreciate response either. He added, "She died quickly. It was a big knife, like a Bowie or Ka-Bar. Took a lot of strength to drive it through her back. Probably gang related."

My mind was spinning. I decided to do the basic cop strategy and say nothing without a lawyer present. I could feel the mood shift in our little talk.

I asked, "Why am I here?"

"You were friends."

"Everyone was Rose's friend."

He spilled it. Finally, the truth. "She had a hand-written note in her pocket. It said, *'Call Glume about the lead.'*

"What?" That surprised me. She had no lead... *or was I the lead?*

"What was the lead, June? What was she sharing with you?"

"Nothing. I have no idea," I lied. "Who did she talk to last?"

"June, I'll ask the questions if you don't mind."

So this was an interrogation. What a dick. The worm asks me to the scene of a dead friend just so he can claim he had a voluntary statement... no Miranda... sneak attack. Asshole.

"Ask away."

"Did Rose share information or something to do with a police matter with you?"

"No... she asked me about a ride-share passenger I transported, but she said it was a dead end. Full stop. End of story... I have to go."

"I might need to talk to you again. You need to make yourself available."

It was time for me to change my mood. I knew I should keep my mouth shut, but that wasn't a thing that was going to happen today.

"Any time... but bring back-up when you do, fucker."

I turned and walked back to my car. I swore I saw a hint of a smile on Jackson's face. He's a good guy. He knows who the assholes are in the department, and he knew Patterson was one of them.

Coronado Island

I was home in twenty minutes. I called Kimberly first. I told her what happened, and that I believed Rose was killed over our serial-killer case. She agreed.

Kimberly replied, "We have our first client, pro-bono of course. Rose's family is our first priority. We do this right."

"So, we aren't playing around anymore, Kimberly. This is serious. Could be severe blowback, or worse."

Kimberly responded like a boss. "Unlimited budget. Unlimited lawyers… find whoever is responsible for this pointless murder and fuck them up, Glume, if one of us goes down, we all go down."

Those beautiful words were all I needed to hear. Finally, a leader. Outstanding leaders are never sensitive. They are seldom popular. But they get the job done.

Now knowing we have a green-light, I asked a question; "Kimberly do you still have a boat?"

"Yeah. I have two of them. One is a large party boat and requires a crew, but the other is a thirty-two-foot Sundancer that I take out by myself."

"Are you okay cruising up the coast by yourself with your express cruiser?"

"Yeah, no problem, I do runs to Dana Point and Catalina all the time."

I gave her some GPS coordinates and a timetable. She read them back to me. We were good to go.

Next I called Raven.

"Mission parameters have changed." I ran down the story. "Not too late to back out. I am going for an extreme interrogation."

"Glume, if somebody murders an innocent cop, it's our job to find them and do what needs to be done. That ain't extreme, that's duty."

"We're private eyes, Raven, not cops or soldiers."

"We're Americans, right? That's enough to make it our job."

I love this guy.

"Then we meet tomorrow as planned. But we're taking it up a notch. You good with that?"

"I'm good with taking it up two notches, Glume, maybe even three. Hell, I'm okay with stripping all the gears and crashing this son-of-a-bitch. I'll see you at the rally point."

"Copy that."

I hung up the phone, stripped to my underwear, flopped on my bed, and cried myself to sleep.

Rally Point – Old Town train station parking lot

Dawn arrived. Crying time was over. Payback time had just arrived.

Raven was waiting in the parking lot when I rolled in. I got out and opened the trunk of my car. Raven exited his truck with a large black canvas bag that he tossed in the trunk.

Raven and I had agreed to dress Newport Casual so we could blend in. I had to take my usual work attire of jeans, boots, leather blazer, and driving gloves up a notch or two or three. I don't always look like trouble. I know when and how to switch to girl mode, and this was one of those times. I wore a Tibi Sport mesh tank and Helmut Lang seamed sweat shorts under an Aviator Nation Bolt zip hoodie. I wore some comfortable but nicely cared for topsiders instead of military style SWAT boots. I let my hair down and topped my head with an Eric Javits fringe pinch straw fedora hat. I don't have a lot of nice clothes, but the clothes I have are stylish and of high quality.

Raven looked sharp. Most days, he looks more like a man who should be on an armored war horse carrying a battle axe. Today he looked like an extra-large upscale Orange County gentleman. His hair was combed and styled. He sported a delicate silk Tommy Bahama casual button up shirt with pleated front twill casual slacks. I don't know men's brands well, but he looked really nice. He sported some beautiful huaraches on his feet, and he replaced his Oakley's with a pair of expensive Persol folders like Steve McQueen used to wear.

He deserved the heartfelt compliment I gave him. "You clean up nicely, for a big ugly fucker, Raven."

He returned the compliment. "You don't look bad yourself for a dolled up two-bit Doro Pesch knock off. I'd consider you hot if I didn't already know you're an asshole."

"I got my own style, big man. But I'll accept your piece of shit flattery."

Standard veteran-style compliments now exchanged, we hopped in the car and sped north to the O.C.

My phone rang. "Glume, Jackson here. You never heard this from me, but we have a surveillance photo on the suspect. It ain't great, but it's something."

"You have my undivided attention, Jackson."

"He's a big man, not my size but big and bulky... maybe six-foot-one and wearing a dark jacket and jeans... He had a stupid haircut... like a mohawk... photo was black and white so that's about it."

102

"I owe you a beer, brother."

"Anytime. Make it right, June. Make it right before the brass buries it."

"Why would they do that?"

"I don't know that they will, but I have that vibe. My instincts got me through Fallujah in one piece and kept me alive on the street all these years. I don't know if that's good enough for you, but I'm still here, so… I just know."

"Good enough for me. Call me if you hear anything else… please… and thank you, Jackson… I appreciate it."

"No problem."

He disconnected.

I briefed Raven on the information. I noticed his jaw tighten. Something about the update bothered him, but I didn't press. We had a job to do.

Orange County, California

Half an hour later, we ditched Interstate 5 at Dana Point and took PCH up to Newport Beach. We made a pit stop at the Crystal Cove Shopping Center and took a bathroom break and picked up some coffees at the little independent brew company rather than from the ubiquitous corporate commie coffee shop next door. I enjoy my coffee being served by an independent businessperson rather than a pretentious knob with no skin in the game.

As walked back to the car, I dumped a half jar of no-doze pills in my cup and let them dissolve. Raven saw me do it but didn't say anything. If I get below a certain level of jacked-up, I get cranky. I'm not a speed freak… it's all legal. The government wouldn't allow drug stores to sell stuff that wasn't good for us, right?

We drove out of the lot and continued north, rolling by the Fashion Island Mall and passing the light at Jamboree Drive. Just before the bridge we hooked a right and wove through the narrow road to the marina parking lot.

According to the file, McHale's boat was tied up at L dock in the Sundance Marina in the Back Bay.

"How do you want to do this?" I asked, deferring to Raven's tactical expertise in extracting terrorists and war criminals.

"Walk down there, drag him out of bed, kick his ass, and get some information."

That didn't seem like the polished covert tactical plan I was expecting.

"We need to be low profile, Raven. This needs to be done quietly."

"No one will suspect a thing. By the way, can you drive a boat?"

"I was assigned for six months to the Harbor Patrol. I can get by with most recreational vessels. Why, are we stealing a boat?"

"Perhaps," he said, while sharing an evil smile.

So, it's time to get evil. Cool!

We retrieved our handguns, a roll of duct tape, and a couple of small flashlights from our war bags in the trunk and walked to 'L' Dock like we owned the joint.

Gaining entrance to slips is fairly simple. The modern marinas all have surveillance cameras and electronically controlled gates that can be opened with a fob or card. I have ride-share contractor card on a lanyard. I simply put that in my hand with the neck strap hanging nonchalantly from my fist. To any monitors or looky-loos, they would see the authorized gate pass-device they expected to see.

Timing is part two of this equation. People come in and out of the dock gates all day, but not in a constant flow. We had to walk, stall, watch, and spot someone either coming or going through that gate. Raven and I stood about thirty-feet to the side, pointing at a particular boat as if we were discussing it until we saw our human pass-key approach the gate.

A commercial diver, one of the guys who scrapes barnacles off of hulls, walked up to the gate with two buckets and the vendor fob. He was happy to let two upscale mariners enter with him as I symbolically waved my hand over the fob reader like I knew what I was doing.

We strolled confidently down the docks until we found the boat. I handed Raven one of my silk scarfs.

If you are a boater, and you see a boat that retails new at over a million dollars in one of the nicest marinas in California, and it looks like a pack of jackals had been camping on deck, it breaks your heart.

There was a week's worth of garbage on deck, everything was scattered everywhere... it was a mess. We stumbled through the debris field. The cabin door was open and I could hear what sounded luck a ruptured bear grunting below deck.

"What the hell is that, Raven?"

"Snoring."

"Sounds worse."

"I've heard worse."

I didn't ask any further questions. I couldn't imagine anything worse.

We tied the scarves over our faces, let ourselves in, and worked our way back to the master's berth. There in all his glory was our subject, the animal-abusing gay communist, unconscious on the big queen bed, spread eagle, and wearing a florescent purple speedo that sort of glowed in the dark. Not a sight I want to remember. I definitely want to erase any thoughts of what those brown and white stains were all over the front of him.

Raven grabbed his foot and yanked his ass off the bed. He hit the floor with a dull thud.

The son-of-a-bitch didn't wake up.

I open palm slapped his belly as hard as I could.

"What the hell!"

Our commie popped to his feet like a rocket. A rocket that was swaying on its launch pad. A rocket that looked like it might pass out again. His eyes started rolling up in his head, so Raven took a cue from me and slapped him hard across the face.

That got his attention.

"Stop it!" he screamed in a high-pitched voice, not dissimilar to a petulant toddler throwing a tantrum.

"We have a couple of questions, partner," Raven said, getting the interrogation underway. "But I think we should talk somewhere more private."

Our target seemed confused, "Huh?"

I answered him by shoving an old sock in his mouth, flipping him on his belly, and binding his hands behind his back with duct tape. I duct taped one foot to a grab rail so he wouldn't run off anywhere.

The keys were in the ignition, so I started the engines and plugged coordinates into the GPS while Raven assumed the deckhand role. We slowly made the long trip out of Newport Harbor into the open ocean. The sea was calm. I opened the throttle and before long, we were fifteen miles offshore.

I backed off the engines to a comfortable six or eight knots and put us on autopilot westbound toward Japan or whatever was out that direction. It was clear motoring as far as we could see. This might take a while.

Raven relieved me at the helm so I could make a head call. I took care of business but there was no soap at the sink. I looked around some cabinets and found the soap. I also ran across a bundle of money. It was about eight grand.

I returned topside and showed the cash to Raven.

"Found this in a locker. I'd like to give it to Rose's family."

He agreed. "Makes sense. Actually, a good idea. We should toss this place and see what else we come up with."

"Take a look around. I need the fresh air for a bit."

Raven searched the vessel like a narc with a warrant. When he returned, he had a big frame revolver, an S.T. Dupont cigar lighter worth north of a grand, and another eight-hundred bucks in cash.

"Nice score, Raven. Find a waterproof ditty-bag and we'll take all this shit with us." I noticed the lighter was monogrammed. It didn't worry me. I knew why Raven would want it.

"Cool."

Forty-five more minutes passed as we headed further out to sea.

We returned below deck to continue the conversation.

McHale was lying unconscious again, legs spread out wide on his big queen bed, one foot still taped to the grab rail.

I made a professional observation. "I think our friend is airing out the family jewels, which is disgusting."

Raven seemed to agree. He started the party by taking a little shuffle step and punching our host in the nuts as hard as he could. I swear I heard an unnerving squish sound on impact. I'm pretty sure McHale heard it too.

His howling scream fell on deaf ears. No one out here can hear it but Raven and I, and I sort of enjoyed it. I think it is safe to say McHale is awake now.

I hopped on the bed on all fours and got in his face. "Here's the drill, dirtbag. I want to know what the hell is happening with the marijuana market in San Diego?"

"The *what*?" he mumbled, still suffering from a hangover, severe stupidity, and a dose of agonizing pain.

"Someone is making moves… people are getting whacked…

Talk to us."

"Killing people is Costa's thing… He's the guy running this shit… I told him not to mess with the Columbians… You are Columbians, right?" McHale said, although in a near stuporous condition apparently from a world-class abuse of drugs and alcohol.

I looked at Raven.

Raven looked at me and shrugged before answering the question.

"Si."

I strained not to snicker.

McHale lit up at the answer. "I knew it. I knew it… Don't kill me and I'll give you everything… Just don't kill me. Okay?"

I gave him a non-committal answer, "I'm listening."

"It worked like this. Costa got the legal shop laws passed. He got funding from the Columbians. I procured a loan from China to finance pushing his bill through last year, so everybody has skin in the game. I'm only drawing ten percent. But once the money started rolling in, Costa said we didn't need you guys anymore. He began skimming and ghosting the calls from Bogota. Then he jacked a load. Then he ripped off his own stash house… A realtor partner guy caught on and he got popped. I never met the realtor guy he was just a local investor and Costa supporter in politics… Costa told me all about it. I think it was a warning. He's crazy. Then the Columbians sent a lady accountant up… she's an attorney too. She got whacked. I knew this would happen… I knew you would come for me."

"Who's doing the killing? It sure ain't Costa," I said.

"He has a goon. Big son-of-a-bitch. Scary looking… some kind of ex-special forces guy. That's all I know. They call him Patch."

The name elicited a visible reaction from Raven. Subtle, but I saw it.

"Where can I find this Patch guy?" Raven asked.

McHale blurted out an answer without hesitation, "I don't know… he's still in San Diego. I think he has another target… I just don't know."

McHale started bawling uncontrollably. I didn't feel sorry for him. But we weren't done. I doubt if he knew about Rose. But I had to ask.

"What about the lady cop?"

"Her? She was a meaningless piece of shit… she dug in and got too close. It was funny. She had to brief Costa, so he had her ass whacked. I guess she got close to something, some kind of lead. The Chief will make sure it goes nowhere. He gets a thousand a week from us."

My jaw tightened, but I didn't let him see how his comment ground a nerve to the quick. It was tough not to kill this prick immediately. "Who killed her?"

"That goon, I guess. Costa just ordered it."

"Which goon?"

"The creepy one. Stocky, mohawk, ugly."

I was surprised and not surprised. He cooperated with us, that was true. But he called Rose a meaningless piece of shit. Fuck this guy. I had what I needed. "I'm done. All yours Raven."

He directed his attention to McHale.

"You got convicted of animal abuse, right?" Raven asked.

The question confused him. "Yeah, what's that got to do with anything? It was just a dog. Stupid puppy was cute… I let it run around my car, then it jumped up in my face on the freeway and almost caused an accident, so I pitched it out the window. It was just a stupid dog. I got another one at the breeders the next day. Why?"

Raven carefully picked McHale up and carried him topside. With careful aim, he smashed McHale's temple against the radar arch, killing him instantly, leaving a plausible cause of death. The news report wrote itself, '*Drunk dipshit boater screws up and gets himself killed at sea*.' We removed the duct tape from the body and cleaned the glue residue off his wrists and ankles as best we could. I wiped everything down to eliminate any prints. We tossed him overboard. Within eight hours, the aquatic residents of Davy Jones' Locker wouldn't leave much for a forensic team to look at.

"I guess we didn't need those masks after all, Glume."

"Better safe than sorry… it could have gone either way."

Raven almost laughed out loud at that one, "Bullshit, Glume. It always goes one way in these things."

Time would be our friend. Evening fog would eliminate most of the evidence of our presence with a thick coat of moisture covering the boat. He would drift away from the vessel and the autopilot would carry the big yacht out another fifty miles before anyone would notice. Raven crawled down into the engine compartment and stuck a knife blade in the edge of the seal around the outdrive so the boat would start to take on water. The opening was subtle enough it might pass for natural wear. I could see Kimberly's boat approaching.

Raven paused and looked me in the eye. "You seem okay with killing, Glume. You kill your share before?"

It was a serious question and was asked as cold and lifeless as a congressman's smile.

I thought about what I wanted to say before I answered. I decided to give it to him straight. "I killed some in the sandbox, some more when I was on the cops, and maybe one other asshole who shouldn't have fucked with me that we shall not discuss again. Not big numbers. Killing isn't my thing, at least not anymore. I'm only okay with it if it needs to be done."

"Killing *is* sort of my thing. Killing and music. Just wanted to make sure we are good."

"We're good, Raven. What happens in Death Metal Investigations, stays in Death Metal Investigations."

He laughed. "Suits me."

We hopped off and swam to her cruiser. The water was cold, but bearable. Ten minutes later we were on our way back to San Diego.

I told her the story.

She was good with it.

CHAPTER 9

Death Metal Investigations

We quietly sat in Kimberly's office. No one talked. We sipped coffee and Bailey's while reading news stories on our phones to see if there was any blowback on McHale.

Nothing.

Our little yacht wanker was such a seeping asshole nobody missed him. His boat was probably halfway to Australia by now if it didn't already sink.

Raven spoke first. "We have a trove of information. Do we give it to the feds, work it ourselves, or run for our lives?"

I jumped in. "We need to work this. Nobody else can be trusted. Even the Chief of Police is in on it. Probably the feds are too… and since when did the FBI ever do anything but feather their own nest?"

Raven countered, "DEA might help. They're mostly good, basically the CIA's annex within the Justice Department, which is why the AG always dumps on them."

"They have a lot of good guys," I admitted. I was thinking about one in particular, a tall, dark, and handsome Agent Luna when I added that comment. And the 'good' I was talking about didn't have anything to do with law enforcement. I squirmed a little thinking about him.

Kimberly sat quietly listening, a faint hint of malicious intent glimmering in her eyes. She was our wild card, our leader… not from the military… not a cop… she was an outsider who thought like a roadie, a problem-solver with no interest in rules, and a *'show must go on'* attitude towards obstacles. Her black cat was curled up asleep on her desk. It appeared a bit sinister too. I don't know why. Purring should erase any sinister vibes. That cat was like a mood ring. It was like a projection of Kimberly's thoughts, and right now her thoughts were dark. Weird.

Our boss closed her eyes as she spoke as if she didn't want to be a witness to the words she was about to share. "*We* work this for now. Brief me every two hours. We don't know who to trust, so trust nobody… and watch your backs."

The big man grumbled, "Fair enough."

I nodded in agreement.

Consensus.

As Raven and I stood up to leave, Kimberly raised a hand.

"I forgot to tell you. I have Mr. Gillespie coming in today. How do you two feel about adding him to the team?"

"How does he feel about working with *us* is the big question," Raven offered hesitantly.

His tone told me Raven felt a bit guilty about how he initially treated our conspiracy theorist friend.

I added, "We could use his skills. An analyst could be a big help with this goat screw and we have a lot of data to sort through now."

Kimberly allowed an involuntary snicker to escape while visualizing a romantic goat interlude. I admit, it *is* a good analogy for our case and it broke the grim overtones of our meeting.

"I'll let you know if we come to terms."

"Cool." I hoped she worked out a deal.

Perry's Diner

I avoid the area of Rosecrans and Midway Drive like the plague. It's overrun with bums. I make exceptions for my favorite drive-through burger joint and Perry's… although a case could be made that Perry's is part of Old Town. Still, the parking lot is plagued with hobos and lunatics.

I wolfed down a big plate of machaca and eggs while Raven demolished a stack of pancakes and a huge omelet.

"You eat like a dude, Glume," Raven observed.

"To many times I've been called away from a meal. When I eat, I eat like I may never eat again. A bad habit I guess."

"So what do we do? We can't go put the bag on the Chief or the Councilman without evidence."

"I'm not sure. We got Columbians on the way. That might light things up."

"No shit!" Raven said between chews.

"Or, maybe we watch Costa and see what happens. We don't

have to nab him. We can just watch him."

"I'm okay with that. How do we find him?"

"I'll call Rose and… shit."

My eyes welled up.

"It's okay, Glume. It will take a while." Raven almost sounded like a human being.

I gathered my emotions. "Never mind, I'll find the little prick. Why don't you get some rest and when I find him, I'll text you a location."

"Sounds good to me. Nothing makes you more tired than open ocean swimming. I slept good but my shoulders are still sore and I'm still sleepy."

We finished our meal. I dropped Raven off at his truck and then flipped on the ride-share application on my phone. I needed to drive.

Ride share journal entry – June Glume

I took a nurse from her apartment in National City to the hospital in Hillcrest. She didn't talk during the ride. She just stared out the window like she had shell shock. Poor lady might have stayed in that job too long and now she can't do anything else. Maybe I'm reading something into it. Maybe she's doped up.

The next passenger was at a Hillcrest diner and was heading back to a hotel on the Bayfront. I spotted him waving me down at the curb, a young guy, nice looking and well-dressed.

"Hyatt," he said breathlessly as he hopped in the back.

I drove while he stared into his phone the entire trip. Nothing.

Some days, you get a lot of zombies in your car. Today looked like it was going to be like that.

I tried one more. I picked up a middle-aged guy at the Midway Museum. It was a run to the airport, terminal one. He started chattering before he got his seatbelt fastened.

"Do you know why it's important to know the value of money? Do you know the value of money?"

"The value is usually written on the front of money, sir. At least it is here in the states."

"What are you, foreign?" he asked, ignoring my answer? "I'm

good with accents. I bet you are from someplace else."

"What airline, sir?" I asked.

"Southwest. I bet you are from around Nebraska."

"Go Buckeyes!" I answered with the first thing that popped into my head, just to shut him up.

"Buckeyes are Ohio. Ohio is a great place. Ever been to the Air Force Museum at Wright-Patterson?"

Is he drunk or high?

"By the way, I'm Bill and I'm in sales. Graduate of USC and the Dale Carnegie course. I've been all over the country and in every industry."

"I never would have guessed you were a salesman," I said, trying to conceal my eye roll.

"Best in the company... I usually fly a charter jet. But it's in maintenance so I have to fly commercial. I never fly commercial but if I do, I fly first class."

"Southwest has first class now?"

"Well, not this trip, but the other trips.... Where did you say you were from again?"

"This is your terminal, sir. Best of luck."

He got out without further conversation... which saved me having to shoot his ass.

I checked the ride report later. He left me a dollar tip. Dick.

- End journal entry

Rejuvenated by my ride-share high, I headed back home to make some calls and freshen up. I didn't tell Raven, but I was sore too.

After a glass of water, a power-nap, and a shot of Jack Daniels, I felt totally renewed. It was time to figure out where Costa was. I did an online search of city council news and discovered he'd be dedicating another new modern art disaster at the Embarcadero. It was almost too easy. I called Raven and arranged to meet him there.

Forty-minutes later, I was a face in the crowd of mostly on-duty city employees watching Costa spin bullshit. He talked about art and how he was an artist, which was absolutely not true. He talked about the Embarcadero and how he was critical to its upkeep, and then he said something about being a musician, so he understood the busker business, which was totally false. I knew it was all lies, but his butt-ranger city hall sycophants sucked it up like little hummingbirds snorting colored sugar-water.

I texted Raven, letting him know it was possible someone in the crowd might recognize me and asked him to take point. I'd wait in my car. Even with my hoodie and shades, I sort of stick out in a crowd unless it's like an Angelcorpse concert, where I would disappear into the masses. Besides, I'd heard enough political-puke-speak for one day anyhow.

Raven called and reported that Costa was heading for the parking lot under the County Building with his security detail. I told him to get a car description and I'd pick it up.

Raven gave me the tag and description, a new black Navigator. I spotted it. It went directly to the city hall garage. I lost them inside.

I made a quick phone call. "Raven. He's gone. Dead end today. We need to come up with a better plan."

"No shit."

Another call came in. I disconnected Raven and picked it up. It was Kimberly.

She blurted out, "Something is going on. Get back to the office. Turn on your car radio to local news."

My boss hung up on me.

Typical.

Death Metal Investigations

Raven beat me back to the office parking garage. We walked upstairs together.

"Sucks to be us," he offered in the way of encouragement. It was not the best pep talk I'd ever received. It wasn't the worst either.

In the office, Kimberly was visibly agitated, as was the cat. The seventy-two-inch TV on the wall was tuned to a local news station. A marijuana dispensary had been burned to the ground and the manager was found dead in the alley behind it.

A grim news announcer read his prompter, "The victim was the manager, a twenty-eight-year-old Chula Vista man, who, according to reports, had his throat slit, which our experts tell us is consistent with the rise in local gang violence. Now more from our field reporter, Brick Stonerock, who is live at the scene."

Raven said it first, "The Columbians are here."

"Scorched earth in 3… 2… 1," I added.

Kimberly was not a fan of gruesome murder. Not that I was, but I made a living off of it at one time. She set her jaw square and gave it to us straight. "If we bump titties with the Columbians, it will likely never end. You can back out now if you want. I'd like to see this through. I'll leave it up to you."

There was never a doubt in my mind. I don't care if it was the KGB, they killed Rose and someone was going to have to pay for that. Columbians, border cartel, Chinese mob… it didn't matter. I wanted to feel the warm spray of their blood caressing my face after I shoved a screwdriver in their jugular.

"I'm in."

Raven was on the same page. "I'm in too. I've dealt with worse."

A deep booming voice from the doorway added to the vote, "I'm in. I have no use for such riff-raff."

Mr. Gillespie was in the house.

The mood quickly melted from cold outrage to a warm greeting.

Kimberly said, "Welcome aboard, sir. We can certainly use your help."

Going against his norm, Raven was exceedingly polite. "It's good to see you again, Mr. Gillespie. I'm glad we'll be working together."

"Me to, Raven. This should be fun."

They shook hands. I guess the corpse of their previous dust up was completely buried in the past now.

I added my two cents, "Welcome aboard, sir. Thanks for joining the team." I reached out to shake his hand, but he took my hand in his and kissed it. He's a charming bastard. It kind of turned me on…

"My honor, Miss Glume."

Kimberly took over. "Mr. Gillespie will have a small office here, but he will remain in his current office except for briefings or as he otherwise determines is necessary."

Gillespie spoke next, "I have some initial findings on the intelligence from… wherever it was you happened to find it, totally above board I suppose."

Raven and I judiciously didn't answer. Gillespie harumphed and continued.

"The data you uncovered maps perfectly to what I was working on. It appears Costa, a Mr. McHale, and one other partner bribed politicians and local special interest groups using money invested by a major Columbian drug trafficking organization and a loan financed by the Chinese government, not unlike what happened in other major U.S. cities."

Gillespie paused to sit and make himself comfortable in one of the leather chairs before continuing, "They controlled what became an instant billion-dollar industry, but there was trouble managing cash. Credit card companies were reluctant to partner with a federally prohibited substance and the banks wouldn't touch it. California wanted to tax it. The plan became complicated."

"So, what happened," Raven asked.

"They established courier systems using unwitting drivers, stash houses using unwitting vacation-home rental owners, and they bought old banks, plus they had a fleet of armored cars."

"So why the couriers?"

"They couldn't haul away all the money and dope with their armored car fleet. Plus, the bulk of it needed to be shipped to a financially discreet location, then redistributed as dividends to the investors. Except someone got greedy."

"Let me guess, the politician?" Kimberly asked.

"Give that lady a kewpie doll!" Gillespie responded with a bit of glee in his voice.

He loved the role of lecturing professor. That much was obvious to everyone in the room. But he was riveting in his voice and mannerisms. His storytelling skills were off the charts.

Gillespie continued, "So our greedy Mr. Costa hired some local thugs to occasionally jack loads of cash. He could safely claim it was just coincidental and could be expected. But Columbians were not blushing debutantes on their first date. They sent a woman who was an accountant and an attorney. She wrote a report. She was on her way to a meeting with a courier who would personally fly the file to Columbia on a private jet. Then she was killed."

"Dead lady on the Embarcadero… messy kill." Raven added.

"There is a gentleman here who took the 'hired muscle' up a notch. This character they call Patch is working for Costa. He was supposed to clean it up.

"What do we know about Patch?"

"Well, if we had fingerprints, I could speak conclusively, but it appears that it is ninety percent certain he is a former convict, ex-military, and sadist named Gerald Rios. He mixes up his method of operation to keep the cops off balance. He's big, about six-foot-six and has a tattoo on the back of his hand that says 'reaper.'"

I might have scrunched up my nose at that one. "Creepy."

"How does Costa know him?"

"Oddly, he met him at the annual comic book convention event. It seems as though Mr. Rios likes Wolverine. So does Costa… which seemed weird."

"That is weird." Kimberly said with a confused expression on her face, or perhaps an expression of disbelief. Either way, she was confounded.

"I guess it's a San Diego phenomenon," I added.

Raven asked, "Wolverines like in Red Dawn? That's my favorite movie."

"No, comic book character who has knife fingers," Gillespie answered.

Raven appeared disappointed.

"How do the cops fit in?"

"Some of the police officers, like six or seven, are liberals or secret pot heads. They supported Costa. He corrupted them, including the Chief. They all get key positions and a stipend every week."

"Sounds like that was way too easy," I noted.

"It's worse than you'd think. People like Costa have been campaigning on reducing hiring standards for years. They get in people who are bright but incompetent and physically weak. Those are the easiest to pick off."

"Wow… I had no idea." I might be kicked out of the cops, but it still hurt to think about a pack of commies infiltrating the department. In hindsight, it made perfect sense. I could probably name them. The Chief was always a spineless political hack. And now I know how a limp-dick-do-nothing like Patterson got into homicide. Thank God for cops like Rose and Jackson… and even Sergeant Bridger. Bridger is a crude asshole, but his blood runs PD blue. Sometimes it takes a few assholes to get the job done. After all, without heartless assholes, who would work motors?

But the big question remains.

I asked it.

"How do we take down a police chief and a city councilman?"

Gillespie smiled. "How does every 'take-down' happen? With a patsy to take the blame."

I saw Raven smile. He might have hurt his face doing it, but as a former sniper he studied Hathcock, Alvin York, Chris Kyle, and I hate to mention him in the same thought, but the nexus of his smile was based on his study of former Marine Lee Harvey Oswald, the godfather of patsies.

Kimberly studied our faces. "You know this is deep shit."

"Rose knew it was deep shit," I answered.

Kimberly handed down her verdict. "If we can't bust them straight up with evidence, we do what needs to be done. I'm sick of crooked politicians."

Everyone in the room nodded in agreement. We were going to evolve from private detectives to vigilantes. I suppose justice is not a fine line, but a broad gray stripe across the hordes of criminal shit stains who stink up the universe. You can't get justice only one way. It's more like that fast-food chain. And we were going to have it our way if necessary.

Gillespie added, "I'll have Columbian files with some photos and phone numbers developed soon. Perhaps that will help."

Kimberly closed. "There is not much we can do for the moment. Let's let Mr. Gillespie work, then we reconvene and wrap this case up."

My head was spinning with this data dump. A chance to even the score with Rose's killers was too delicious to let it slide by. I needed a drink.

CHAPTER 10

Drinking alone is the best drinking. There is no risk of criticism regarding your behavior and you can work at your own pace.

I overdid it though.

I have a bit of a photographic memory. I consider it a curse rather than a benefit. But I was struggling to recall exactly my last words to Rose. I can remember everything I see and hear, but not everything I say. I had been pointlessly mean to her. I'm abusive. I should die.

More alcohol.

Did you know Vodka in Russian means water?

More alcohol.

Unconsciousness.

Awake to puke.

More booze. I mixed it with some orange juice for health purposes and to kill the barf taste lingering in my mouth.

Restless sleep.

A phone call stirs me from my melancholy binge.

It was Raven. "Glume, Gillespie has a plan. Come to the office."

He disconnected without waiting for my answer. I wanted to call in dead.

I wasn't sure if I could get out of bed. Shit… I wasn't in the bed. I was on the couch. What the hell? My head hurt.

I made coffee and ephedrine for breakfast to jump start my heart.

Two cups later, I began to recover a minimal sense of self-awareness. I knew I was a mess. I knew I had to get my shit together. I knew it wasn't going to happen.

I started to call Raven to tell him I'd be in later when I saw I had a text message.

Oh hell no.

I drunk texted Luna.

He answered by suggesting we meet for coffee sometime. His response lacked any enthusiasm. I wondered if he even knew who I was… I wondered if I was mental.

As much as I wanted to see him, I didn't want to interact with any Feds while this case was underway. I'm such an idiot.

I sent him a text telling him I was sick and asked for a rain check. I followed up with a text to Kimberly telling her I had the Russian flu and wouldn't be in for a while.

I ate some ibuprofen and a piece of bread.

Back to bed.

A day lost is a day never seen again.

I'm a dumbass.

Day and Night Diner - Coronado, California

So after another six hours of sleep, I could pass for human if not examined too closely. I sat in the diner wolfing down a breakfast burrito and coffee. I needed to absorb the last remaining vodka molecules in my system and to do that requires a big hot plate of Mexican food.

I'd be able to go home after this, finish flushing out my system, then re-shower, re-dress, and head to the office before three in the afternoon. For a burned-out vet and private eye, that is called punctuality.

I tipped Julio ten bucks. It was nice having the cash to be able to do that for a change. After the pit stop at home, I hopped in my car and drove to the office.

Everyone was there, merrily working away… the pricks. I still had a headache but was functional.

Kimberly gave me the evil grin of a boss who has you by the balls, "Now that we're all here, I'll turn this over to Mr. Gillespie."

Thankfully, Gillespie kept it brief and to the point. "The Columbians have a six-man team in town. They seem to be unclear on who needs to be killed so they are starting at the bottom and working their way up. Technically, we could sit back and watch the show. But I think we might want to be more involved in the demise of Mr. Costa and our corrupt Chief. Keep in mind, they will be reluctant to whack the chief, and I'm not sure if they are even that interested in him, but you never know how fast and high they will escalate their rampages. The Columbian cartels and Mexican traffickers certainly kill a lot of police chiefs in their respective countries. These particular Columbians are staying in Hotel Circle, remaining low profile. Here are the packets on four of them. One more is at large and unknown."

Raven raised his hand, "FYI, I don't like the Columbian cartel guys either."

Gillespie did not comprehend the direction of that point but answered as best he could. "Not a problem. I'd say they are free to shoot at will, to the extent you think you can get away with it."

Gillespie is a hard-assed little fucker. I like that in a man.

"We need to make sure we get to Costa first and leave their stench at the scene," I added, feeling a little surly and self-righteous. When I have a bad hangover, I get self-righteous sometimes.

Raven gave me a wink before speaking. "Give us the address on the Columbians. Glume and I will go for a drive."

Gillespie handed him a file folder with the information and some photographs.

It was time to get to work. I'd have to put my ride-share gig on hold until this was over.

Hotel Circle, San Diego, California

We found the hotel with our foreign hit team and did a little 'on-foot' recon of the area. There was a steak house next door. If they didn't have food delivered, they might show up there. We needed a clean count on their numbers and a schedule. That requires patience and an ability to blend in. So a hulking scary giant and a chick who looked like Metallica's sound crew might catch someone's attention.

We bounced over the nearby mall and I picked up a cheap blazer and a pair of leather sandals at the low-end department store. I dodged into the restroom to change out of my leather jacket and boots, brush my hair, and dab some make-up on my face. I came out looking like a visitor from Indianapolis.

Raven took the car, and I did the reconnaissance on foot. My first stop was the lobby.

All it took was a quick glance around the room to find what I was looking for.

A chunky dark complected man was reading a magazine in the corner. He was well groomed with slightly long slicked-back black hair, nicely dressed in a black suit, and was sporting a nice gold

Rolex GMT Master II on his left wrist. The cop in me noted that he might be right-hand dominant. His shirt was open and he sported a couple of fat gold chains around his neck. Did I mention he was packing a handgun under his coat? That's the part that made him noteworthy. As I came through the door he stood up to buy a bottled water and I could see the imprint. The way he moved indicated he was a professional. I maintained a scrutinizing eye on him like a mother duck watches her ducklings.

He had to be in the lobby as a lookout. I surreptitiously snapped a photo of him with my phone and sent it to Raven and Gillespie.

I found a chair in an out of the way corner and chilled in the lobby for an hour, trying to look as if I was waiting for someone. No one paid attention to me, so I felt pretty good about my cover.

A text message from Gillespie came in.

'You are watching a dangerous man. Hector Villarosa. Cartel assassin. Careful.'

But after fighting the Taliban in Afghanistan, I wasn't sweating a gun thug from Columbia. Hector is the one who should be careful.

Another player showed up and replaced Senor Villarosa. He was bigger. He wore jeans and work-boots with a black polo. Something about him smelled of sadist. I snapped and sent his photo.

I followed the dapper Hector back to his room. Eighth floor.

He knocked and someone opened the door for him. That accounted for three. One in the lobby, Hector, and the guy who opened the door.

I hopped on the elevator and pushed the button for the basement. In most of these joints the basement is where the employees report. There was a rack of white kitchen shirts, so I scored one and went to the kitchen. There I swiped a cart with food prepped on it. Then I returned to the eighth floor. I let my hair down and walked stooped over with my face slightly turned away.

I banged on their door. "Room service."

"We didn't order anything. Go away."

"This is compliments of the manager." I insisted.

The door flew open and a new guy came out and told me to beat it.

I caught a glance inside. three guys were sitting around the table. I memorized their appearance but couldn't take a photo. And now there were five, three table guys, door guy, and lobby guy.

"Get the fuck out of here," the goon at the door growled.

I persisted with my ruse. "No, no, no… I must deliver this and have you sign for it."

I tried to bum rush the door and force my cart in around him. I think he was surprised at how strong I was and I got inside a little further. He muscled me back out. I picked his pocket, a skill I learned during a year-long tour in vice.

Now I was burned for close-surveillance. They'd recognize me if they saw me again. But we verified Mr. Gillespie's intelligence packet and we knew who we were dealing with.

I left the hotel and called Raven.

He answered brusquely, "Yeah."

"Confirm five guys. There is the possibility of more, but I think we are safe to say five. We'll need to find another eyeball for the lobby."

"Should we send in Gillespie or Kimberly?"

"I think we need Mr. Gillespie at the computer running analysis. Call Kimberly. I'll meet you in the parking garage."

I met Raven at his car on the third-floor level of the parking structure. His parking spot provided at least a partial view of the entrance. It would have to do.

"Hey big guy, guess who has a wallet fresh from Columbia." I snickered showing him my big score.

"No shit? Did you pick his pocket?"

"Yep. It's a rare little skill that comes in handy more often than you would think," I bragged.

Raven pontificated. "Asshole skills, when used for good, are valuable skills."

I'd never heard Raven make such a philosophical remark before.

I announced the next steps. "I'll dump this thing, photograph the contents, and send the pictures to Mr. Gillespie. Call Kimberly and see if she is comfortable holding down the fort in the lobby until we decide how to use this."

As he made the call and explained the mission, I hopped into the back seat and took apart every shred of the wallet. I photographed the front and back of each item of the contents, even the currency. Gillespie can do some of his magic with the new analytical and investigative algorithms and other metaphysical computer guru dark arts.

"You got a cloth?" I asked.

Raven continued with his phone call as he dug into the console and handed me a micro-fiber that he uses to clean his sunglasses.

First, I changed back into my real clothes, black jeans, leather jacket, and SWAT boots. Vets aren't shy about things like that. Raven didn't even attempt a glance at my Venus-like figure. Which wouldn't have been weird if he did. Besides, he likes big busty women who can carry a stolen car transmission at a dead run and I prefer men who are a little more evolved down the evolutionary scale, men who own a razor and have six-pack abs instead of guys who are built like an angry and violent Idaho potato.

I wiped my prints off of everything and reassembled the wallet. I kept the money. It was around three-hundred bucks. Mr. Assassin could buy us lunch a nice lunch.

Using the microfiber cloth, I stuffed the wallet on an inside pocket of my jacket and then I wiggled to jam the cloth into my pants pocket. Tight jeans might show off my fine-looking ass, but at times like this, I wish I had on cargo pants.

Last step into my transformation was pulling back on my black leather Red Wing Heritage driving gloves.

Ahhhhh… Finally, feeling normal again.

Forty minutes later, Kimberly rolled up and parked beside us.

"Hey guys, didn't think I'd get in on the fun this soon. Let me see the pictures of these turds."

I showed her the two faces we captured on my phone and advised her, "No contact and super low profile."

"No problem."

She headed out for her assignment.

An hour and two coffees later, she called.

"They're on the move. They don't have their suitcases… I don't think these clowns are checking out. I'll follow them out front and get you a direction of travel."

Raven whispered to me, although it was unnecessary to whisper. I guess he automatically switches into his tactical mindset when dirtbags are on the move. "I got them. They're coming our way, heading to the garage."

I notified to Kimberly that we had them and sent her back to the lobby to wait until we are all clear from the hotel. No sense getting the boss killed or arrested. She didn't know what Raven and I were going to do for a reason, and that reason is that you can't tell the cops what you don't know. Deniability.

Kimberly responded. "Got it… heading back in. I got a picture of the group. I'll send it to Gillespie."

Kimberly should have never gotten out of her lobby chair to follow the targets outside when they left, and she *definitely* shouldn't have immediately turned and walked back into the hotel talking on a phone, but this wasn't the time to explain that to her. I kept it positive. "Good. Wait inside until they leave the area. We might need you again." I didn't mention that I needed the person who signs my paycheck to avoid death. We could cover the tactical errors in a debriefing later.

Raven slid out of the driver's seat. "I'll walk down and identify their vehicle. Take the car and pick me up. Keep the line open."

"Copy that."

Professionals know intuitively to frequently change up the team members on foot in a surveillance.

Three minutes later Raven reported, "Black Impala rental car is leaving the garage. Four guys. That means one of them is at large."

Shit.

I called Kimberly and blurted out an urgent command. "There are only four in the car. One more is still out there somewhere. He might have made you and doubled back. Get out! Now!"

An accented male voice answered me. "She is with me now, my little room-service maid. Now get your ass back here. I want to know who in the hell you are."

He recognized my voice and he had Kimberly… my excellent plan just turned to excellent shit.

"Who is this?" I asked, buying time, trying to keep the door open to negotiation.

"I'm the man who will cut the throat of this pretty young lady… Now like I said, get your ass back here. We will have a little chat about why you are watching us."

I disconnected and peeled out of our parking spot, speeding down the circular exit ramp gaming the centripetal force to my advantage while fighting inertia as I accelerated through the turns. I spotted Raven at the main exit near the hotel entrance as I blew out of the garage.

"Take the car, I'm going after Kimberly.

Raven didn't get in the car. Instead, he leaned in my window.

"Stay with the targets," he ordered, "I'll take care of this."

I realize the tone of my voice hints I'm approaching a near panic state. I try to conceal it. "No… you stay with the others. This asshole is expecting me." I was livid at my poor judgement in allowing Kimberly to be placed in jeopardy and not asking her for a head count when the bad guys left.

Raven didn't budge. "Listen, I don't want to sound rude, but I'm qualified for this and so is Kimberly. She's fine. Give her some credit. I wasn't just in Delta force, June. I was a bass player in a heavy metal band. She was a roadie. We've both been in worse spots."

His logic seemed like it should be flawed, but it wasn't. As an Army vet and ex-cop who occasionally listens to Pantera, I get it.

"Fine. I'll follow the mobile assholes. You deal with the ones in the hotel."

Trust your team. Have faith in your teammates. It ain't as easy as it looks. It's like flying into a fog bank and relying on your instruments to get you through even though you feel like you might be going the wrong direction.

I left a patch of rubber blacker than the skid mark in Bin Laden's shorts after Seal Team Six rolled up on him in Abbottabad as I burned out of the garage and pursued the bad guys to a destination as of yet unknown.

Hotel Room Hallway

Raven walked down the hall with the purpose of a man eager to deliver bad news to an enemy. He pulled a Glock out of his belt and kicked the bad guy's room door off of its frame.

As the door exploded into the room, Kimberly hit the deck. She was untied, so she flattened herself on the floor.

The Columbian hit-man was lying on the bed staring at his phone when a nine-millimeter bullet tunneled through his forehead and out the back of his neck. His death face bore the dull expression of a parent who found a turd in the baby's diaper.

Raven sneered at the lifeless body. "Life comes at you fast, dirtbag!"

"Raven, what took you so long?" Kimberly asked.

Raven thought he heard her giggle. "Why did you let yourself get kidnapped?"

She was grinning like a kid who just discovered farts make bubbles in bathtubs… "Inexperience and indifference, big man. I'm here for the fun. I haven't had this much excitement since we opened for the Dead in Phoenix and a riot broke out."

"Yet, here you are, closing for this Dead at Hotel Circle…" Raven directed a thumb at the deceased maggot on the bed. "Is it the glamor that attracts you to this life, Kimberly?" Raven gave the back-and-forth eye glance between her and the dead cartel hood.

"Something like that… but we should go help June… She's got four-to-one odds against her. And there is another guy out there… These assholes assumed I didn't speak Spanish… I speak Spanish, Italian, and some Portuguese, oh and…"

"Good for you, now let's go!" Raven cut her off impatiently, not fond of loitering at murder scenes.

She persisted. "There's more. They talked on the phone about a DEA guy at the Fiesta Island dog park. Some Fed named Luna… I overheard one of them say the Fed would have a black German Shepherd and that he always walks it out there at Mission Bay after the end of his shift around eleven. But what was weird was, they were talking about someone killing the agent, a guy who works for Costa… I think they have someone on the inside with Costa's people"

"What?"

"Yeah… one of the others complained that killing the DEA guy was bad for business… at least that's what he said… they kept mentioning an assassin named Patch… I don't think they know him firsthand. They have photos Patch and of the agent on the table."

"Patch… are you sure?" Raven focused his attention to the photos on the coffee table. One was of a fairly handsome guy and the other was someone he knew well… big, ugly, mohawk… Patch… the deserter. Raven set his jaw, clamming up and attempting to conceal his visceral wrath from Kimberly. "Yeah, we'll ask June first if this is part of our deal. First, you wipe the room down for your prints. I'll dig that bullet out of the couch. Take his gun too. And any loose intelligence you find. I'll keep these photos."

"What about video surveillance?"

"I'll hit the security room on the way out. It will take five minutes. These hotel companies won't use cloud storage for liability reasons, so they probably have a couple of hard drives. A bottled water will fix that."

"Let's get to work."

Santa Luca Luxury Residences – North County, San Diego

I spotted the four Columbian hitters and followed them towards Oceanside. Fifteen miles outside of the downtown area, they hooked a right-hand turn off the freeway and went into a resort community in the rolling hills north of downtown.

I'd been there before on a case. The sprawling golf and tennis luxury development had gate guards at every entrance.

I lagged back until I could determine which entrance the Columbians were using, then followed through after them, far enough behind they wouldn't get the idea there was a tail.

I prepared a bullshit story as to why I was there as I passed through the gate, but I wasted my time creating a scam story to get inside. The security guy was already dead and stuffed under a desk.

These Columbians don't mess around.

I saw their taillights ahead in the distance and noted that they pulled into a cul-de-sac and went dark.

I called Raven.

"Hey!" he barked.

"Hey, yourself… did you get Kimberly?

"We just finished up. Where are you?"

I data dumped him the address.

After giving them a minute to load the location into their map application, I continued. "I think they are up here to whack somebody. I'm not sure who lives up here though that might be their target."

"We're on the way.

"Copy that."

I waited. The bad guys just sat in their car. I wasn't sure what they were going to do, but it looked like bad news.

A few cars came in and out of the cul-de-sac. From what I could see, there might be fifteen homes on the street. But no activity from the Columbians indicating who or what they were waiting for.

Ten minutes passed when Raven and Kimberly arrived all full of piss and vinegar.

They parked behind me and then exited their vehicle, hopping into my car.

"Hey Glume!" Kimberly shouted gleefully.

"What did you assholes do, have an armpit smelling contest or are you just high on life?" I asked.

She spilled out an overly excited summary of their activities. "We had a harrowing experience. Raven saved my ass… but we reduced the population of Columbia by a factor of one."

"Whoa… you whacked that guy?" I asked.

Kimberly was unusually amped. She's typically very laid-back, perhaps one of the most laid-back people I know, but I guess after being the victim of a kidnapping and subject of a brutal rescue, she was adrenalin dumping like it was free.

"I have his gun," she blurted out as she showed me the Baretta nine-millimeter.

"Shit. So you *did* kill him."

Raven answered. "Somebody did. My recollection of the details regarding this incident details are a little foggy. But we got a hot lead. There is a wild-card bad guy who might be the asshole who killed Rose. He works for Costa. He's going to try to kill a DEA guy tonight at eleven. He's going to do it at the dog park on Fiesta Island.

"Son-of-a-bitch…" I glanced down at my Glycine Airman wristwatch that my dad wore in Viet Nam. That gives us two hours. But he's mine. I'll do that one. You guys keep an eye on this."

I felt myself starting to have some kind of anxiety attack over the possibility of finding Rose's killer.

A more composed Kimberly spoke, now the calming presence, distracting me from my hyper mode. "We can do both. Time is on our side for a change…. Let's process this shit. What do you have?"

"Four bad guys percolating in the car." I pointed out the shadowing vehicle parked away from the houses.

Raven snorted, "You can almost smell the murder on them."

"Yeah, I've seen this kind before. Cartel guys, Taliban, organized crime ass wipes. They all got that spilled shit-bucket vibe."

Kimberly spoke up again to ask a very pertinent question. "So do we shoot them or what?"

"We wait. We see who their target is. Then we decide."

I was dying for a cigarette. But fortunately, I was amped up enough with war vibes that I didn't need ephedrine or uppers to stay buzzed. We were witnessing what will probably be an epic shooting gallery. But before we intervene, I need to know if I *want* to intervene.

Raven whispered, "Lights!"

Front lights, probably either motion sensors or timed illuminated the front lawn of one of the massive estates.

"Raven, hand me my binoculars. They're in the glovebox."

Raven dug into the compartment and passed me the compact 16-32 field glasses I used to carry in my cop war bag. I glassed the brightly lit yard.

"Shit."

"What?"

"It's the fucking chief of police."

"Shit."

"Yeah, and four other guys. All wealthy looking ass-hats."

The tone of Kimberly's voice hinted at concern. "What do we do."

I took a deep breath before passing a death sentence on the corrupt dirtbag who fired my sorry ass, the rat bastard who wouldn't stick up for one of the troops when the chips were down. A guy who let a good cop like Rose get killed and wasn't willing to do anything about it but blame it on gang violence and file it forever as a cold-case. "We watch."

"Movement," Raven warned.

The hood car didn't turn any lights on, it just started and slowly rolled up on the men in the yard.

Typical.

It stopped directly in front of the house.

Normal procedure.

Four men quickly exited the vehicle, their movements as coordinated as a military unit.

Professional hitters.

Each had an MP5 sub-machine gun with a silencer.

Yikes!

I heard some poor clueless slob in the yard cautiously ask, "*Can I help you?*"

The guys in the car did not seem to require any help. They just opened fire like they were spraying for weeds.

In the length of time required for a thirty-round mag-dump, all the yard men, including the corrupt police chief, were sprawled out dead in the grass.

Then the Columbians went to work.

Machete time.

The quartet of violence hacked away at the bodies with all the unbridled fury of the devil making soul sausage. In Bogota, they call that *sending a message*.

Then Kimberly opened her door to puke.

The interior light came on.

We were spotted.

"Shit."

I'm unclear on which of us said it first, but I'm pretty sure we can all be quoted as saying the same thing.

"Shit!"

Luckily the Columbians didn't immediately reload after their fireworks show and they were ten yards from their car where I presume the rest of their ammunition was stored. That brief few seconds was all the time we needed.

"Haul ass, Glume!" Raven squealed like a pants-pissing second-grader on all you can drink chocolate milk day… which I hope is a real day.

He wasn't afraid, he was laughing like a teenager on a rollercoaster.

I yelled at Kimberly, "Clean that puke up. This is my ride-share car. I usually charge fifty bucks for a puker." I was more put out than I should have been considering what we just witnessed and knowing that as tough as she was, she wasn't used to mass murder and body desecration.

I knew the local roads and I strongly suspected that the bad guys didn't. By the time they got to their car and reloaded, we were long gone. I gave it ten minutes and doubled back. My partners' ride was still there.

We can't leave a company car at the crime scene. That could be bad for business.

I pulled in behind their car. "Get your car and get the hell home," I ordered, not really being in charge, but being the only one who still had something to finish tonight. "You two need to get far away from this."

"What about the four guys?" Kimberly asked.

"These assholes will leave town immediately. They don't like witnesses. They'd usually invest whatever time it takes to kill us. But they don't know who we are. So they'll bail.

Kimberly didn't let it go. "What about the DEA guy?"

"I'll go get him. I'll take care of everything and meet you back at the office."

Raven volunteered a better plan. "June, let us help. You hired me to help with the ugly stuff, and it's going to get really ugly. You can't do both things alone."

Kimberly was confused. "Two things?"

I said my next words carefully. "We have Columbian assassins on the rampage. That leaves their next move open to creative interpretation."

"What?" she asked.

Raven knew what I had in mind, but Kimberly was lost. She was still a decent human being.

I continued, "And give me that dead guy's gun."

She retrieved the weapon and handed it over.

"I don't *even* want to know," Kimberly said, sensing my intent.

"Correct. You don't."

Raven made a suggestion. "Glume... let me get the DEA guy. I'll make it right with the dirtbag who killed Rose. You're the only one who can do the other thing. Who do you *really* want, the hitter or the guy who ordered it?"

As much as I wanted to rescue Luna and be his hero for life, and maybe his main squeeze, I knew his situation was custom designed for Raven. I was torn about wanting to get revenge for Rose. But I could get revenge at a higher level. The rogue assassin was just a tool. I wanted the dirtbag responsible.

"Get Kimberly to safety then go save Luna... and may God have mercy on our souls." I said that last part somewhat facetiously to lighten the stress, but Raven took it very seriously, almost as if he had another mission of his own.

"No shit, Glume… because there won't be any mercy in San Diego tonight."

CHAPTER 11

Fiesta Key, San Diego, California

It was a beautiful night in dog park. It was late enough that no one else was there. That's why the senior DEA agent went there. After a shift of dealing with the worst humanity has to offer, some alone time with his dog helped restore his soul.

Agent Luna picked up the dog after work and was enjoying their nightly dog park stroll on Fiesta Key. He took the leash off Vlad's neck and let the black Czech Border Control bred German Shepherd run free.

Luna found a large flat rock to sit on while he smoked a cigarette.

He didn't hear anything.

But he wasn't alone.

A big man with a mohawk had been waiting in the shadows.

Luna stared at the water. Maybe he'd bring out his jet ski on his next day off, he thought.

He never heard the man with the knife approaching from behind.

The man with the knife never heard Raven.

A big man who can move fast generates a lot of power. When that power is focused into a flying drop kick between the should blades, the man on the receiving end is at risk of a broken back.

Mohawk man flew forward twelve feet into a hard-scrabble face plant. But he wasn't out. He rolled and got to his feet, squaring off against his opponent, a man who looked strangely familiar.

Luna pulled his duty weapon. He didn't know who to shoot or what the hell was going on.

Raven threw a left hook, right hook, left uppercut combination. Each blow pounded Mohawk man. He should have gone down. But he remained on his feet, absorbing the blows.

A right overhand lead connected to Raven's cheek.

Raven responded with a brutal side thrust kick to the solar plexus, driving Mohawk back and preventing him from following up with a counter-attack.

The kick doubled up the killer as he sucked for air. Raven followed through with front snap kick to the face, straightening him back up, and then spinning him around and throwing him into a police choke hold.

Mohawk knew he was in serious peril. He struggled wildly as Raven applied full pressure, compressing the carotid artery and shutting off oxygen to the brain. Raven shouted at the DEA man who was now getting to his feet, "Agent Luna, he's a contract hitter. Don't shoot me! I'm a friend. June Glume sent me."

"Who the fuck are you," Luna challenged as he waived his weapon at the two combatants, unclear as to what the hell was happening.

"US Army veteran and friend."

The shouting drew the attention of another warrior who had been out on the shoreline hunting rabbits. From the darkness, Vlad the shepherd, sensing Luna was in trouble, decided now was a good time to join the fight. The one-hundred-and-five-pound dog hit both men with a glancing blow as he flew through the air like a fur missile, knocking both of them off balance. The courageous dog attacked almost six-hundred pounds of beef without hesitation.

Mohawk saw an opportunity as Raven's attention was divided between him, the dog, and the armed agent. With a free hand, he threw a desperation groin shot with his right fist into Raven, connecting effectively and loosening Raven's grip, followed by a series of elbow strikes. A left elbow connected solidly with Raven's temple.

Raven went down stunned and seeing stars.

The huge thug spun around and kicked Vlad hard as the big black shepherd came back for another pass, connecting with the canine hard enough to knock it out. Mohawk executed a forward shoulder roll, retrieving his knife, and charged Luna who was now less than three yards away.

It wasn't Luna's first rodeo. He pumped five rounds at the big killer, after all, the bastard kicked his dog. That made him a bad guy… and a man with a knife within ten feet is a righteous shooting, a no brainer. Snap firing at point-blank range. He had to have a few hits on target.

But the assassin was one mean son-of-a-bitch. His momentum

carried forward, and he buried the knife into Luna's right shoulder in spite of being on the receiving end of three non-lethal gunshot wounds.

Sometimes it takes a lot of ammo to drop a monster.

Luna was down on his back.

The hired-killer slapped Luna's gun away and kneeled down on one knee, raising the knife one more time to finish the job before he risked bleeding out.

But before Mohawk could deliver the final fatal stab, the assassin felt Raven's smelly armpit smear over his head as Raven applied a mixed-martial-arts guillotine choke hold around his neck.

"Remember me, Patch, you filthy deserter?" Raven increased the compression, twisting the killer's neck around so he could see who was about to murder him out of the corner of his eye. "You sold us out to the enemy then ran… what did they give you? Money? Dope?"

The assassin known as Patch blinked once in recognition, trying to wrench Raven's death hold off his neck, sucking for air.

Raven had him. "Yeah, it's your old pal Sergeant Francis Marion Ravinski. One of the soldiers you left to die back in Afghanistan… but bad news, Patch… One of us got out of there alive."

The assassin's eye's widened in recognition as Raven leaned back increasing the torque on the hold and snapping the killer's neck with a sickening crack. Raven tossed Patch's lifeless body off to the side and checked on Luna.

"You okay, agent?" Raven asked as he pulled a cloth handkerchief from his pocket and shoved it into the knife wound.

"Who the hell are you?" a confused and seriously wounded Luna asked. "Is my dog okay?"

Raven explained as he ripped a strip of cloth off his shirt and wrapped it over the handkerchief in Luna's wound forming a crude but effective bandage. "I told you I was a friend, dumb ass. This dead asshole was a hired killer working for one of your local elected officials. They put a target on your back, brother. They knew you were an honest cop and wouldn't let this case go."

"No shit." Luna groaned as Raven kept pressure on the wound.

"No shit is right… and I'd like you to count to thirty before you call 9-1-1. It would be my preference to not be involved… as in *never here*… as in *doesn't exist*. You know, an unidentified concerned citizen."

The dog regained consciousness and limped over to lick Luna's face.

Raven commented, "That's a good dog. It put its life on the line for its master. Can't ask for better than that... So I wasn't here, okay?"

"Fair enough. I owe you that much," he agreed as he hugged the happy dog with his good arm.

Raven dabbed at Luna's wound one more time. "You'll be fine. Nail all the bastards behind this mess, Luna. Four Columbians are heading for the border tonight in a black Impala four-door. I think they did most of your dirty work for you already."

"You got it."

Raven got up to leave, "No problem."

"And thanks, man... I'm damned lucky you were here."

"Luck wasn't part of it. I've been looking for this piece of shit traitor for two years."

The streets of San Diego

I love to drive. I prefer to be alone when I go for a spin. Tonight was special. I *had* to be alone. I was going someplace dark, dark as my black heart.

Driving allows me to reflect on things that matter to me. Driving at night is the best for that process. Thoughts flow and swirl around that special place where the range of the headlights fades and the black darkness of the night world provides a hypnotic, romantic, perhaps a bit psychopathic part of my soul to flourish.

Someone was going to regret taking a dump on June Glume's parade. Political corruption can't be tolerated. We make enough mistakes without being sold down the river by dirty cops, especially those at the top of the food chain. Our weak-kneed commie chief was now a fine example of a fully rehabilitated snake. I reflected on him lying comfortably on a grassy lawn shot and hacked to pieces. Call me sentimental but I think he got off easy. I hated that lying dirtbag.

Dirty politicians who create dirty cops are the lowest form of crawling insect life... total scum.

Then I thought of Rose. She was pure and honest as god

intended cops to be. Of course she was a bit whiny and frumpy, but that unique character, flawed or not, is what makes a detective. Detectives are like snowflakes, each one different and each one special in its own way.

Detectives know things.

Detectives aren't the winners and they aren't the losers in the legal system. They are the eternal knights of justice, not law, but justice. If patrol cops are society's guardians, repelling the enemy at the gate, the detectives are the hunters, tracking down the worst animals of society and making them pay for their evil ways. Payment might mean a clean bust and conviction. It might mean a bit of street justice. It might mean straight up revenge. I am virtually certain some dead child-molesters buried in the desert are compliments of your ever-loving boys and girls in blue. Not judging. Sometimes justice might come down to the right lifer in prison receiving a few cartons of cigarettes and a name.

Good versus evil. The cops never win. They never lose... they're just there, holding the line.

I miss being a cop. I can't admit it to anyone else, really. But I do. It was my life and I loved it. I loved the banter, crude remarks, jokes in briefing, action, back-ups, fights... it was a lovely career.

And Costa ended it.

He shook down my friend at the burger stand for fifty-bucks this month.

I don't like him.

He started the wheels in motion in a double cross with the Columbians that led to a lot of innocent people getting killed.

I despise him.

He ordered the murder of my friend.

I hate him.

And now I'm parked a block from his house.

The drive was over. The reflection was over. Rose was still dead and her children and husband still grieved.

I got out and walked to his front door. I opened the lock with my pocketknife.

I could hear a sound resonating from within.

Snoring.

He was sound asleep in the ground floor master bedroom.

I walked in and turned on the light, abruptly interrupting this piece of shit's peaceful slumber.

He snapped upright in shock… startled and rubbing his eyes before he became clear headed enough to recognize me.

"Glume? What the hell do you think you're doing? I'll have you thrown in prison forever for this, you stupid bitch!" He raged while pulling his covers up to his chin like a kid who thinks a monster is under the bed. But this time there *was* a monster, and that monster was me, an ex-cop with a dead friend and no compunction about taking out a corrupt murdering political hack.

He sat there in shock as my black leather-gloved hand raised a deadly weapon.

Now wasn't a time for chit-chat or speeches. It certainly wasn't an ideal time for Costa to call me a bitch. So I kept my choice of words short and sweet. "This is for Rose, councilman."

"It's council*person*!" he instinctively corrected my politically incorrect farewell.

Famous last words. Go woke, get smoked.

I popped him between the eyes. His melon smacked against the headboard as the slug ripped open the back of his head like a bottle of muscatel ripping through the bottom of a cheap paper bag.

"And this is for me."

I shot him in the groin. Twice… then one more… and one more. *Yeah, I feel better already.*

I wiped down the smoking handgun Kimberly stole from the dead assassin in the hotel and tossed it on the floor.

I also dropped the wallet I lifted when I pickpocketed the guy at the hotel room door with my fake maid routine.

Frame set, match, point. Dirtbag slug murdered by cartel assassin.

I quickly scanned of the room for any lingering evidence when noticed a black leather bag on the dresser. Feminine curiosity required me to examine the contents. Oh my, it was full of cash. I wonder where that came from?

He won't be needing it now. Is stealing off a dead guy a crime? I don't think so.

It was a beautiful evening.

I strolled back to my car.

I felt pretty good about myself.

Self-esteem level… high.

Regrets? Not a fucking one.

Death Metal Investigations - Coronado, California

"June, where did you go last night after that fiasco," Kimberly asked cautiously, clearly not sure if she wanted an answer.

"Home."

"Really?"

"Why wouldn't I go home?" It is my policy to start answering questions with questions upon being pressed over a lie.

Mr. Gillespie wisely changed the subject as he scanned the local newspaper. "Interesting article I read this morning. Four foreign nationals detained at the border and weapons were seized. The authorities believe they were Columbian. And this headline is fun, gang violence suspected in death of beloved police chief and councilperson."

Raven smiled. "You don't say."

"I do say. I just said it," Gillespie countered.

"Figure of speech," Raven muttered as he flipped off Gillespie.

Gillespie leaned back in his chair, basking in the knowledge that he won the debate, "Bite me."

I'd heard enough. We were definitely a team now. And we were ready. Good times were definitely ahead. But I needed to drive. "I'll see you all tomorrow morning," I said to the group in general as I got up to leave.

"Take a week off," Kimberly said. "Everyone."

"Cool," Raven said as he got out of his chair and headed for the door.

Kimberly wasn't done, "However there will be mandatory happy hours every night that you will required to attend. I call it post-case mental therapy."

"I like that name," Mr. Gillespie said with a wide smile. "A week will give me time to work up the files on our next case."

"Next case?" I asked, as I stopped in the doorway.

Kimberly put her hand up. "It's a major hard-rock band that has a problem with an organized crime extortion ring. We meet them in Miami in two weeks."

I smiled, "Fair enough. Right down our alley."

I got up and left. It was time to hit the street. I needed to feel the texture of the steering wheel, yell at street corner bums, and flip off other drivers... at least I'd flip them off when I didn't have a passenger on board. That's my therapy.

Ride share journal of June Glume

I picked up a few tourists. No one was chatty. No one buried their nose in a cell phone. They just enjoyed the sights of America's finest city. It was a pleasant change.

I saw a trip from a Little Italy Hotel up to the Point Loma Lighthouse. I took it.

A young guy hopped in. He seemed nice.

"First time here?" I asked. I usually don't start conversations, but I was in a good mood.

"No, I come up every year. I like to sit up there and read. I'm from Iowa."

"Really? That sounds like the makings of a nice day. Usually people come to San Diego for the comic book convention or to get drunk and puke in the Gaslamp Quarter."

"No... not for me. When I got out of the Army I got a degree in engineering. I never have time to look at beauty or reflect. That whole stop and smell the roses thing. And also my grandfather is buried up there on the hill. He was a sailor. I walk over there and visit him."

"What do you read?"

"Bronco Hammer books. I'm sentimental, not a pussy."

"World's most dangerous writer." I added. "He's the best."

I drove up the sloping hill and dropped off my new favorite passenger.

Unlike Diogenes, the eternal wanderer of the ancients, I finally found an honest man. I guess life is better than I remember it being.

One more stop to make.

I ran by Rose's house. I parked in the driveway. I retrieved an item from the trunk and knocked on the door.

Jerry answered.

Rose's husband.

He was crying, but he tried to hold it back.

We hugged.

"Thanks for coming by June. Rose loved you."

My damned allergies started acting up. I fought it.

"Rose might have mentioned to you that I work for some philanthropists now doing security and they took up a little collection." I handed him the leather bag I stole from our late councilperson… I forgot his name already. Shame.

"Thank you, June. It means a lot. Times are tough without her salary. I'm so screwed. The kids and my job. I can't afford a nanny. Every little bit helps.

He has no idea how much a million-and-a-half might help.

I gave him a kiss on the cheek and got to my car before he opened the bag. I knew he wouldn't open it in front of me. He wasn't that kind of guy.

Some days are better than others.

Epilogue

Death Metal Investigations – a week later

Raven leaned back in his chair facing his boss, "I got good news and bad news."

Kimberly took the bait. "What's the good news?"

"I scored a gig with a band. I'll be going back on the road."

"What's the bad news?"

"I have to leave the company. Not that I want to. You need to know how much I appreciated this gig, Kimberly."

The gratitude and regret were obvious on his face.

Kimberly sighed and smiled understandingly. "In a way, I'm envious. I wish I could go back on the road with you… but that's not my life anymore." She paused then stood up and offered her hand, "Raven, you always have a job here. The door remains open."

Raven uncharacteristically smiled and shook her hand. "Thanks, I appreciate it, Kimberly. I don't know how long this new gig will work out, so I may take you up on that."

"It's going to be tough to find a replacement. Do you know any big bad sons-of-bitches looking for work?"

Raven laughed. "I've never met a man as bad ass as me,

Kimberly… June comes closest, but she's already on the roster. If I run across a candidate, I'll give them your number."

June Glume's Apartment, Coronado, California – ten days later

My phone rang. It was an unknown number. I took it anyway. What the hell.

"Glume?" a masculine voice deeper than the Mariana Trench asked.

"Yeah."

"It's Harold Jackson."

I knew exactly who it was when I heard that Isaac Hayes voice on the phone. Officer Harold 'Slam' Jackson. The big man. A street monster… the one guy at the PD who had my back when Rose was murdered.

"Good to hear from you, brother."

"Glad you are still doing okay, little sister. I was calling to tell you that I just put in my retirement papers."

"So you finally pulled the pin… the streets will never be the same. Congratulations Slam. You had a great career," I said, using his nickname.

"Thanks, June. I appreciate that… but I wanted to ask you something. A favor."

"Sure."

"I heard you had a detective agency. Could you use another guy? I still got some work left in me. I ain't ready for a straw hat and fishing pole yet."

"Meet me at the Bird's Nest Café in Coronado, big man. I think we need to talk."

The end

About Bronco Hammer - Author

Bronco Hammer, a son of Texas, is a mysterious and complex individual. He currently spends his days enjoying a cold beer, while authoring action novels at his current home in Coronado, California. He doesn't have a cat. That is about all you need to know.

Oh... You think you need to know more? Fine... His interests include trucks, boats, horses, guns, happy hour, sandwiches, and science.

Order action novels by Bronco Hammer at **amazon.com/author/broncohammer**

Stay in Touch

Bronco Hammer can be contacted at the **Bronco Hammer Briefing Room** at *broncohammer.com*

About Dan - Senior Creative Consultant

After retiring from a twenty-three-year law enforcement career, Dan focused his attention on various endeavors that remain classified to this day, mainly because he forgot most of them.

What readers are saying about action novels by Bronco Hammer

Chris Jones - Before I started reading Bronco Hammer books, I was 5'4" tall and weighed 422 pounds. I was physically and mentally challenged. After my first read, I grew 7". Then after my second read, I grew 6 more inches. I lost 150 pounds, and now am a brute with testosterone oozing from almost every pore in my body. I have had to hire bodyguards to keep women at bay. And I have only read two of his books. Actually, I am scared to read a third book. I may need to arm myself then.

Michael Babb - Before I started reading Bronco Hammer books I had E.D. Now, every time I open one I get a raging boner.

Carl Skornik - Before reading Bronco Hammer books, my confidence with women was at zero. I am now at a solid 1 and can walk around with most of my clothes on.

John Craig Williamson - You're books have cured my cat dander allergy! *(Author's note: I don't have a cat!)*

Mike Cardis - Just last week I finished my first Bronco Hammer novel. My cojones grew 3" in diameter OVERNIGHT. My doctor said it's pancreatic cancer but I told him to shut his Commie Pie hole.

Gregg Girard - Oh no! She told me that she wouldn't let that book be released.

Scott Joseph - Life does become a Hai! Karate commercial.. I was a Mensan BEFORE I read the books. Now I'm dismissing Einstein's theories as trifling...

Jeff Trapp - After dropping Bronco's weighty tome on my head, I

145

believed that all of the book's manly knowledge had been magically transferred to my brain since I had a sizable swelling in my man bits. As it turned out it was just a priapism from my head injury. Luckily, the head injury wing at this hospital is located in the "Bronco Hammer Nymphomania Treatment Center."

Terry Porch - Bronco Hammer books should be published with very bold HAZARDOUS WHEN READING labels.

Panthea Caldwell Baker - This is Bronco Hammers cat. He continues to deny me as his feline! I feel so confused! (author's note: NO CAT!)

Carl M Miller - "Who needs Viagra® when you've got Bronco Hammer© books?"

Jacque Trapp - My dog ate my Bronco Hammer book and now he won't leave my other dog alone. Anyone want a puppy?

Кимберли Кали - Even sexy women read Bronco Hammer novels. I'm on "Dead Guy In the Alley." Maybe I'll even try this hairstyle in the morning after reading this.

Gary McIntyre - All TRUE!

James Klingaman - When I got my first Bronco Hammer novel I was nearly seventy years old. After reading it, I was literally in my 40's again with the stamina of a twenty-year-old. As for ladies, I was flocked and turned all away unless they agreed to change their hair style to look like a Hammer Cover Girl.

Edgar Tolmie - Bronco Hammer books contain 98.7% more macho than other leading book brands.

Earby Markham - Bronco Hammer, you mean that guy that writes the non-fiction books. Yes, that stuff really did happen. I know. I was there. Now kiss off